MORNING SUN IN WUHAN

MORNING
SUN
IN
WUHAN

BY YING CHANG COMPESTINE

CLARION BOOKS
An Imprint of HarperCollins*Publishers*

Clarion Books is an imprint of HarperCollins Publishers.

Morning Sun in Wuhan
Copyright © 2022 by Ying Chang Compestine

ISBN 978-0-35-857205-3

Typography by Samira Iravani
22 23 24 25 26   PC/LSCC   10 9 8 7 6 5 4 3 2 1

First Edition

TO MY BELOVED HOMETOWN—WUHAN

CHAPTER ONE

山雨欲来风满楼

The raging wind precedes the coming storm

JANUARY 19, 2020, EVENING

It feels as though hours have passed since the waitress took my order. As I scroll through photos on my phone, part of me still expects a text from Mother to pop up.

Mother:
Where are you, Mei?
Finish your homework before
playing computer games.
Meet me at Double Happy for dinner?

How can the world exist without her? My eyes dampen when I come across a selfie of us. We were making rice cakes that day,

1

and I patted flour on her face until she looked like a geisha. We laughed until my stomach ached.

The woman at the next table puts another garlic shrimp into her daughter's bowl. Mother wouldn't have done that. She would've peeled the shrimp before giving it to me. Now that I think about it, she would have never ordered a shrimp dish with the shells still on.

The girl doesn't look up from her phone; she keeps pounding her thumbs on the screen, probably playing a silly, mindless game that doesn't require skill or strategy. The woman catches me staring and smiles at me. I blush and avert my gaze to the window, looking past the four large red lanterns swaying in the wind. They cast a blanket of ruby light over the restaurant's entrance.

Thunder rolls in the distance. Dark clouds are gathering over the hospital compound where Father works. From across the street, it looks like a big factory. Patients are lined up along its thick brick walls — more than usual, it seems.

Finally, the waitress with red lipstick appears, holding a round tray over her shoulder. She must be new, as I have never seen her before. I ordered Mother's favorite dishes: lion's head meatballs, stir-fried spicy lotus root, and steamed Wuchang fish — a sample of Double Happy's signature dishes. The waitress's head dips as she sets the dishes down, exposing the white roots of her hair.

"Need anything else?" she asks.

"No, thank you." I use my confident voice and avoid her questioning gaze.

She stumbles away, no doubt wondering why a thirteen-year-old girl ordered so much food, only to eat alone.

The familiar smell of chili peppers in the lotus root and pungent black bean sauce over steamed fish brings back so many memories. The days when Father worked night shifts, Mother and I would meet here for dinner. She would come directly from work, still with indentations on her cheeks from her surgical mask. When I teased her, saying she looked like a Wuchang fish, she would suck her cheeks in and flap her lips. Grunting like a monkey, I would puff my cheeks and pull my ears. Our laughter always drew attention from the people around us.

"Eat a bit more," the woman urges her daughter. The girl doesn't respond, eyes still glued to her phone.

How many times did I act like that when I was here with Mother? If only I could have one more meal with her, I would never ignore her again. Like a song on loop, I can't stop replaying that dreadful day in my mind. I was so happy when I first received the text from Mother.

Mother:
I'm running late and canceled your piano lesson.

I smiled, glad I had more time to improve my ranking on

my video game, *Chop Chop Chef.* In the midst of cooking for my soldiers, who were furiously fighting zombies, Father burst into the apartment sobbing. I didn't—*couldn't*—understand what he said that day, and even after a year, I still can't comprehend it.

I put a few slices of lotus root in my mouth. The chili burns my tongue. I quickly take a bite of the meatball. Its mild taste neutralizes the sting. Did Chef Ma cook these? With the tips of my chopsticks, I pick up a piece of the fish's belly; Mother always served it to me, saying it was the most tender part of the fish. With every bite, I hear her voice.

"Chef Ma makes the best meatballs. Eat more of the lotus root; it's good for your skin. Taste the fish; it's from the Yangtze River. We are lucky to live in Wuhan."

It's been a while since I feasted like this. By the time I've made a big dent in all the dishes, the restaurant is packed. Finally, I get my waitress's attention and ask her to pack my leftovers.

Father will probably work late again tomorrow. The leftovers will be a nice dinner for me. During the rare times I do see him, he is always staring at his phone. Will he work late every night? Maybe I should have gone to live with Aunty.

Even though I don't blame Father for Mother's death—like Aunty does—I can't help but wonder if Mother would still be here if he hadn't always been busy at work, leaving her to run around and do everything.

More families trickle into the restaurant, and raucous parties fill up the two big, round tables in the middle. We used to meet Aunty here, but I haven't seen her since I refused to live with her after Mother's death. Aunty has been upset with Father ever since he discouraged Mother from quitting her job at the hospital to work in Aunty's private pharmacy.

The memory of Aunty screaming at Father after Mother's funeral is still so vivid.

"She should have never married you!"

My thoughts are interrupted by retching coughs. It's my waitress, now standing in the middle of the aisle, a few tables down from me. One hand holds my take-out boxes while the other stifles her coughs, smearing her lipstick into a red mustache. She stumbles a few steps forward, then breaks into another violent coughing fit. The bustling restaurant falls silent and everyone's eyes fixate on her.

Suddenly, she collapses facedown on the floor, motionless. The boxes slip from her hands and break open. A few meatballs roll under the tables, and the dark sauce stains the red carpet. The restaurant erupts like a geyser; people spring from their seats, chairs jostle, and utensils clatter to the ground. Panicked voices slice through the air.

"Doctor! We need a doctor!"

"She could have the new virus!"

"What's that?"

"It's deadly. It's contagious!"

Everyone swarms to the front door. I grab my bag and slip out the back.

Cold rain drizzles down and quivers under the streetlights. I shiver and pull up my hood, running past the growing line of patients outside the hospital. A thousand questions race through my mind as I hurry home. What just happened in there? Will someone take the woman to the hospital? Is she dead? What "new virus" were they talking about?

Surely, Father has to know; he is the director of the respiratory care department. Then again, is he even home?

When I open the door, I hear the sound of a drawer closing in Father's office.

"Hello, Mei." Father rushes out into the living room.

"You're home!" I exclaim.

He glances at his watch. "I'm leaving in a minute."

"What?" I kick off my shoes, slamming the door behind me. "Where are you going this late?" I struggle to stay calm and throw myself on the sofa without taking off my damp coat.

Mother would have disapproved. She always insisted that I leave my coat in the entryway, but Father doesn't seem to notice. He points to a pile of masks on the coffee table in front of the TV.

"From now on, wear a mask when you go out. For everyone's safety, give one to each of your classmates and teachers."

"Safety from what?"

"I can't talk right now." He dashes to the door and turns to look at me. "Sorry. I'll explain later. Make sure to wear a mask!" He closes the door quietly behind him.

It's flu season, but there is no way I am going to be the first to wear a mask and get teased at school. And what will my classmates think if I randomly hand out masks like a street peddler? Where is he going now? When I visit him in the hospital, I always notice the young nurses flirting with him. They blush and twitter like birds around him. Is he secretly dating one of them?

My eyes land on a photo on the TV stand. The frame is made of heavy green bamboo, as though to protect the memory inside. I reach out and pick it up. Mother captured the moment just before I threw the snowball—my first one to successfully hit Father. I could tell he was laughing even though our faces were silhouetted by the lit-up snow sculpture behind us.

At the beginning of our snowball fight, I made mine too big. I could barely throw them a few feet, and some even crumbled before leaving my hands. Father laughed and teasingly called them "wimpy shots."

I was frustrated, but when I watched how he made them, I figured out my mistake. I took my time packing the powder into perfect, persimmon-size balls. On my third try, the snow held its shape until it smashed into Father's forehead. He cried out, sank to his knees, and fell back.

Mother and I giggled as we ran over to help him up. His eyes were shut, and snow slid down his face, leaving snail-trails of freezing water on his skin. I stopped giggling when he remained motionless. Suddenly, his eyes flew open, and he dragged us down. We shrieked with laughter and rolled around in the snow like three happy bears.

That night, we went to Harbin's famous Ice Restaurant. We waddled inside like penguins in our heavy winter jackets, shivering until our waitress brought out the restaurant's signature spicy beef noodle soup, steaming hot. We competed to see who could slurp noodles the loudest, and forgot we were eating on tables made of large ice blocks.

Since Mother's death, Father has changed so much. I can't even remember the last time he smiled. He used to play his erhu after work. I wonder if he will ever touch it again.

Sad and exhausted, I put the picture back onto the TV stand and drag myself to bed. I pull the covers tight over me, wishing I could choose my dreams. I would dream of our family's last vacation in Harbin.

But instead, I dream of the coughing woman, holding a stack of take-out boxes, stumbling toward me.

CHAPTER TWO

孤雁出群

The lonely goose flies from the pack

JANUARY 20, 2020, MORNING

Bang. Bang. Bang.

Someone knocks on our door. Am I dreaming? I groan and shove my pillow over my head. The knocking grows louder. My thoughts move slowly. I force my eyes open, jump out of bed, and then run to the door. It's our nosy neighborhood community director, Mrs. Fong. Every time this middle-aged woman opens her mouth, words gush out like water from a broken faucet.

"Oh, Mei, what took you so long? Are you okay? Your father asked me to check on you. Why haven't you left for school? Why didn't you come to our neighborhood banquet last week? Didn't you receive my invitation on WeChat? You need to keep up with our neighborhood group chat."

I rub the sleep out of my eyes and remember seeing something in the neighborhood chat about a cooking competition a week ago. For a brief moment, I thought of bringing my signature spicy pork ribs, but discarded that idea quickly. Since Father would most likely be at work, I knew going by myself would have meant answering endless questions from the neighborhood's old ladies:

"How are you coping without your mother?"

"How is your aunty? We haven't seen her since your mother's death."

"Is she coming for a visit soon?"

"I am fine." I force a smile. Mrs. Fong's eyes narrow. I don't give her a chance to continue and say quickly, "Thanks for stopping by. Sorry, I need to get ready for school."

"Message me if you need anything!" Mrs. Fong says as I close the door.

I drag myself to the kitchen, only to find the refrigerator bare. When was the last time Father went to the market? Mother would have never left the refrigerator empty. She always stocked it with soy milk, eggs, seafood, meat, and vegetables in season. I quickly get myself ready for school, and run out.

I check the time on my phone. I already missed first period. As much as I dislike third period—Political Studies—and the teacher, I would hate having to write self-criticisms even more if I skipped it. Despite Father paying little attention to me, I can usually count on him to wake me up for school. I guess he's too busy for that now. Did he really ask Mrs. Fong to check on me, or was she just being her nosy self?

I rush to school, which is six long blocks away. The line of patients waiting outside the hospital now snakes along the sidewalk. Some sit on plastic chairs, resting their heads on their arms, while others crouch on spread-out newspapers on the sidewalk. I can hear their coughing from across the street. Has Father been treating patients all night?

Once I turn onto the main street, it's another scene. Crowds fill the stores on both sides of the street. The loudspeakers blare out promotions for the Spring Festival. People roam in and out, carrying loads of colorful gift bags. When I reach Victory Road, I hesitate, then turn left to take a shortcut through the Golden Seafood Market.

I soon regret my decision. The market is packed. It sells a lot more than seafood. Vendors cry out for customers, waving goose-feather fans over their array of goods. Everywhere I look, there are wicker baskets full of vegetables, bamboo cages with fluffy chickens, fish bobbing in big tanks, and fat eels squirming in plastic buckets.

Shoppers heft bags of vegetables and cuts of meat, shoving through the narrow paths between the vendors. At one stall, a young man is chopping up a large fish on a wooden board. An old lady shouts at him, "Enough, enough! Don't cut it that small."

I squeeze through the crowd and finally make my way out. Down the street, I can see my school. The small compound looks out of place in one of the city's oldest neighborhoods. I walk past ramshackle huts, lined up side by side, with thin walls and tin roofs covered with plastic. Freshly washed laundry hangs on bamboo rods, flapping in the wind.

If Mother hadn't treated the principal's grandson for his smog-induced asthma, I probably wouldn't have been admitted into the newly built Yangtze Middle School, which ranks second-best in Wuhan. I sprint toward the tallest building, a three-story brick structure in the middle of campus.

My Political Studies class is on the top floor. The bell rings just as I open the door, and thirty pairs of eyes land on me. Many of them have probably been here studying for hours before school even started. I slide through the narrow aisle to my seat next to the back window.

Even though we are still in middle school, these over-achievers already act like the Gaokao—the rigorous National College Entrance Exam—is tomorrow. I couldn't care less about getting into top colleges. If only I could convince Father that my destiny lies in culinary school.

"Good morning, class!" Teacher Wu, with his watermelon belly, wobbles up to the podium. "Did any of you attend the Ten Thousand Households Banquet?"

A dozen hands shoot up. Am I the only one in the world who didn't attend the neighborhood banquet?

"You should all feel very proud and lucky to live in this

prosperous city." Teacher Wu pulls down the projection screen. "As far as I am aware, we were the only city that held this many Chinese New Year banquets. This is the time for us to remember our revolutionary heroes. Without their sacrifices, we wouldn't be able to enjoy today's good life. I will now show you a short video. But first, does anyone want to share what your family made for your banquet?"

The class erupts as if someone dropped water into a wok full of hot oil.

"My mother made big steamed meat buns!" says a boy with chubby cheeks.

"My family spent two days making a huge Chinese flag with red hawthorn berries," a girl with long bangs says excitedly. "My mother and I used orange slices to make the yellow stars!"

"Well, can any of you guess what my talented wife made to showcase our love for our motherland?" Teacher Wu turns on his computer and waits.

"Kung pao chicken!" someone shouts.

"Butterfly shrimps!"

"Rice cake!"

Teacher Wu smiles, lightly tapping his fingers on the podium, obviously enjoying this guessing game.

"What is it? Tell us please!" says the girl sitting next to me, batting her long fake eyelashes.

Teacher Wu starts a video.

An anchorwoman with big eyes and curvy eyebrows appears on the screen. She speaks in a cheerful, high-pitched voice.

> "Comrade Zhang from the Hubei provincial
> government found time in his busy schedule to
> attend our Ten Thousand Households Banquet!"

The camera shows families dressed in festive red clothes, crowding around a large, long table piled high with food. It zooms in on the dishes: noodles topped with minced meat, spicy pork ribs garnished with green onion, steamed fish, fried shrimp, and sweet rice wrapped in lotus leaves. A little yellow flag sticks out of each dish with the name of the family that made it.

> "Comrade Zhang will present the prize to the
> winner of the cooking competition . . ."

The camera pans to a big, round sponge cake displaying a mural of the Yellow Crane Tower, a landmark of Wuhan, painted on with black sesame icing, surrounded with peony flowers made of colorful frosting.

A broad-shouldered man in a suit hands a giant rice cooker to a stocky woman in a red apron. Teacher Wu stands beside her, beaming from ear to ear. The large crowd cheers and claps.

The class bubbles with excitement.

"Wow!" says one boy with a bowl cut.

"The cake looks so good!" says Fake Eyelashes.

Teacher Wu beams.

Bored, I look out the window, where a baby and mother bird are perched on the bare branches of a tree. Why are they still here? Mother told me winter in Wuhan was too cold for birds. If she were still alive, I would have attended our neighborhood banquet with her. What dish would we have brought? Would we have won the competition? As annoying as the neighborhood ladies are, they always complimented Mother on her cooking.

My thoughts jump to my after-school plans. I will do my homework while eating dinner and then spend the night playing *Chop Chop*. Since it was released two years ago, I've been obsessed with the online game, in which players cook for soldiers who guard a walled city against zombies. It lets me practice cooking techniques, try out new recipes, and improve my speed.

"Mei Li!" Teacher Wu throws a piece of chalk, hitting the edge of my desk. "Where and in which year did our People's Volunteer Army win a war against America?"

He caught me daydreaming again. I need to practice looking more attentive. When did he finish bragging? What is he talking about now? Vietnam or Korea?

"Vietnam, and . . ."

The class breaks out into laughter. Fake Eyelashes rolls her eyes and raises her hand.

"Korea, 1953." She smirks at me. I glare at her.

Teacher Wu frowns, then turns back to his chalkboard, droning on about the Civil War between communists and the Kuomintang. He raves about the young revolutionary hero Liu Hulan, who chose death over surrender and was beheaded by the Kuomintang soldiers. Soon, my gaze finds the window again. I start to think about my last game of *Chop Chop*. What could I have done differently? Maybe I could have used less time boiling the noodles. I might have the worst grades in this class, but I bet I could out-cook all my overachieving classmates.

Finally, the bell rings. As I dash out of the classroom, I hear Fake Eyelashes chatter excitedly with two boys about studying together during the Chinese New Year break. Is that what they do for fun?

CHAPTER THREE

天有不测风云

Life is as unpredictable as the weather

JANUARY 20, 2020, MIDAFTERNOON

The second I open the door to the apartment, a sweet pastry smell tickles my nostrils. I open a red paper box on the coffee table. Inside are my favorite treats: egg tarts, deep-fried durian, and osmanthus rice cakes. Bags of corn puffs, shrimp chips, and spicy rice sticks crowd the sofa.

I go to the kitchen, where fruit, instant noodles, bags of rice, flour, and beans are scattered on the counters and floor. Is Father throwing a party? Who will he invite? Since Mother's death, no one has come to visit. Maybe he wants to introduce me to his secret girlfriend. The thought sours my mood.

I open the fridge to find its shelves stocked with food. My spirits lift as I examine the ingredients: bok choy, lettuce, green onions, cabbage, baby back ribs, tofu, thick lotus root, ground beef, fresh shrimp, and chicken breast. There is enough food for me to cook a banquet. With just the shrimp alone, I can make three dishes: shrimp lettuce cups, honey walnut shrimp, and shrimp dumplings.

Father can't even make instant noodles. Is he expecting me to cook for his guests? That doesn't make any sense. He always discourages me from cooking, telling me to focus on academics instead. I close the refrigerator door and notice a note stuck to it.

MEI,

THERE IS A NEW VIRUS OUTBREAK IN THE CITY. IT'S VERY CONTAGIOUS AND DANGEROUS. STAY AT HOME AS MUCH AS YOU CAN AND AVOID CROWDS. I SAW YOU HAVEN'T USED THE MASKS I LEFT YOU. YOU MUST WEAR ONE IF YOU GO OUT. I NEED TO STAY AT WORK FOR A WHILE. CALL ME IF YOU NEED ANYTHING. REMEMBER, DON'T GO NEAR THE HOSPITAL UNLESS IT'S AN EMERGENCY.

YOU USED TO LIKE MAKING THOSE BEAUTIFUL SHRIMP LETTUCE CUPS WITH MOTHER. I HOPE I BOUGHT ALL THE RIGHT INGREDIENTS FOR YOU.
   —FATHER

New virus? Are the patients outside the hospitals all sick with this virus? Is that why Father has been working late? He has seldom mentioned Mother since her death. Does he miss her cooking too? He doesn't want me at the hospital because of the virus, or is there another reason?

I pull out my phone, open the search engine Baidu, and scan through the news feed. One article refers to the virus as coronavirus, a mysterious respiratory infection, and says a few people have died from it and hundreds more have been sickened from it. I scroll down and find another article. It says the virus is like SARS and will disappear when the weather gets warmer. Why is Father making such a big deal about this?

Maybe I should go visit him to find out what's really going on. If those young nurses giggle like little girls around him again, I'll scowl at them until they back off.

A pang of hunger suddenly bursts inside me. I only took a few bites of school lunch. The stir-fried pork was too chewy, and the scallion pancakes were as bland as cardboard. I remember what Mother used to say: "You can't face the world on an empty stomach."

My eyes land on a pack of instant noodles. If I weren't so hungry, I would make myself a bowl of authentic spicy beef noodle soup, just like the one from the Ice Restaurant. But today, these noodles will have to do.

I set a pot of water on the stove to boil and open the bag of instant noodles, then toss away the chemical-filled seasoning packet. Mother said, "Prepackaged seasoning is for people who can't cook. If you put your heart into it, you can transform instant noodles into a gourmet dish fit for an empress."

I heat a few tablespoons of oil in a small frying pan, then sprinkle in some black sesame seeds and dried chili flakes. As soon as the sesame seeds release their nutty fragrance, I crack two eggs over them. When the eggs form golden, lacy edges, I grip the pan, flick my wrist like a badminton player, and send them into a somersault. They land in the pan with the brown side up. I picture myself as the energetic, self-assured female chef in *Chop Chop*, moving with confidence and grace. When the water comes to a boil, I drop in the instant noodles. The hot steam fogs up the kitchen windows.

I throw in a handful of prewashed spinach and splash on a spoonful of dark soy sauce. The smell intensifies my hunger. I stir in a small drop of miso, a sprinkle of white pepper, and a dash of sesame oil. Finally, I flip the crispy eggs on top of the noodles and turn off the heat.

The rising aromas of fried egg, nutty sesame seeds, and cooked noodles deflate my table manners. I grab an oven mitt, carry the pot to the living room table, and dig in.

At the first sip of the spicy, salty broth, the warm soup layers my tongue in flavor, travels down my throat, and blossoms in my stomach. After I wolf down an egg and half the noodles, my energy returns.

The wailing of sirens scatters my thoughts and draws me to

the window. An ambulance's tires screech, and I see a blur of white metal and flashing red lights hurtle past the people waiting at the hospital's entrance. The line breaks apart, and they crowd behind the van, craning their necks to get a closer look. A horde of doctors and nurses in white coats rush out the front doors, stretchers in hand. I open the window and stick my head out to get a better view. Murmurs break out around me. I look and realize I'm not alone. My neighbors are also watching from their windows.

Motionless patients are lifted out of the ambulance, onto the stretchers, and carried into the hospital. I shiver, but not from the cold.

SPICY EGG RAMEN

Makes 1 serving

HERE'S WHAT YOU NEED:

1½ cups water

1 package instant ramen noodles

1 cup prewashed baby spinach

2 tablespoons soy sauce

1 tablespoon miso (optional)

¼ teaspoon white pepper

1 teaspoon sesame oil

2 Crisp Sesame Eggs (see page 24)

¼ teaspoon minced fresh red chili or dry chili flakes

1 tablespoon minced green onion

HERE'S WHAT YOU DO:

In a small pot, bring water to a boil. Add package of instant ramen noodles and discard the seasoning packet. Cook until noodles are soft, about 3 minutes.

Reduce heat to low. Add spinach, soy sauce, miso (if using), white pepper, and sesame oil.

Place Crisp Sesame Eggs on top and garnish with red chili and green onion. Serve hot.

CRISP SESAME EGGS

Makes 2 eggs

HERE'S WHAT YOU NEED:

1 tablespoon cooking oil

2 teaspoons black or white sesame seeds

⅛ teaspoon dry chili flakes (optional)

2 eggs

1 tablespoon minced green onion

¼ teaspoon ground white pepper

2 tablespoons soy sauce

HERE'S WHAT YOU DO:

Heat cooking oil in a medium nonstick skillet over medium heat and swirl to coat. Sprinkle in sesame seeds and chili flakes (if using). Cook for 1 minute, or until sesame seeds release their nutty smell.

Crack two eggs into the pan. Cook until egg whites are crispy and brown on bottom and yolks are firmly set, about 3 minutes. Use a wide spatula to flip the eggs and cook until the whites turn crispy and brown on the other side, about 2 minutes.

Sprinkle green onion, white pepper, and soy sauce over the eggs. Simmer for 30 seconds, turning the eggs once to coat both sides with sauce. Serve on top of Spicy Egg Ramen or by itself.

CHAPTER FOUR

节外生枝

New branches emerge, creating additional complications

JANUARY 21, 2020, EARLY EVENING

I sit cross-legged in front of my desk. Outside the window, a V-shaped flock of wild geese glides past the bare tree branches into the last bit of dimming winter light. Wind whips around the building, and the window whistles softly. I touch the base of the lamp next to my laptop. Instantly, a warm, orange-yellow light casts over my bedroom.

I open Discord, a gaming discussion board, and a message pops up.

DragonMing:
@EmpressMei: Ready to play?

EmpressMei:

Just us? Where's Hong?

I met Ming and Hong last year when I entered Wuhan's annual youth gaming competition. Most participants in the *Chop Chop* division entered as a team, but I entered alone, so the tournament organizers randomly assigned me with the two boys. It turned out we were all seventh-graders but at different schools. Although we only placed fourth, the judges said we could do better if we learned to play as a squad. Since then, we've been practicing daily to prepare for the next regional competition.

TigerHong:

I'm here.

@EmpressMei: Can I pleeease be

your sous chef today . . . 😳

EmpressMei:

@TigerHong: Do we have to go

over this every game?

You need to improve your knife skills first. 😳

Ming will be my sous chef and you'll

be the kitchen assistant. 😄

Sometimes we don't see eye to eye—especially Hong. After the tournament, we fought over what to name our team, so I challenged them to a single-player matchup in *Chop Chop*. Although the game is timed, the dishes must be well prepared, or the soldiers will refuse to eat. If the soldiers become too hungry to fight, zombies will take over the city.

Ming and Hong taunted me for my slow speed, but I ignored them and took my time cooking my dish. They finished before me, but Ming's soldiers rejected his chicken soup, saying it was too salty. When a speech bubble appeared over Hong's general, I laughed so hard I fell off my chair.

General Ironhead:
Chef, we would rather be eaten by zombies
than eat your exploded chicken guts. We will
feed you and your chicken to the zombies.

Hong had forgotten to clean out his chicken intestines. In the end, zombies swamped their cities while my well-fed soldiers danced in victory.

Another message from Hong pops up.

TigerHong:
@EmpressMei: Why do YOU always
get to play the head chef? 😠

EmpressMei:

Because I don't want us to be
eaten by zombies. 😵 🥏

Upon my victory, I named our team the Phoenix Group, after the mythical nine-headed bird with long flaming wings. It was historically used to represent the people in our province of Hubei for their resilience and cleverness.

Without Hong and Ming, I wouldn't have made it through the past dreadful year. With Father always at work and Aunty not speaking to me, many days I feel like an orphan. I knew they had done some digging online about my family when Ming once commented that my father was one of the best doctors in Wuhan. I told him I wished I didn't have a legendary father because he is always busy. I appreciate that they don't ask me many questions unless I volunteer to share.

I met Hong and his parents once at the night market. They all have the same stout build. I've never seen Ming's parents. When I went to his house, I only met his grandmother, a small lady with gray hair who always smiles when she speaks. Ming told me his father is American and his mother is Chinese and they travel a lot for work.

TigerHong:

Ready to play? 🕓

DragonMing:

Ready!

I pull on my headset and log in to the *Chop Chop* lobby. Ming's and Hong's icons are already lit up. I press Start. A cheerful melody, accompanied by the sounds of spatulas scraping woks and cleavers chopping meat, blasts into my headset. I wince and turn down the volume.

A small timer appears on the top left corner of my screen. The moment the numbers start counting down, three characters jump into a kitchen. My avatar, the head chef, wears a waist apron ornamented with red phoenixes over her black outfit. She flips her braid over her shoulder and grabs a spatula and cleaver. I have decided that once my hair grows longer, I will braid it like hers.

The sous chef and kitchen assistant stand in position at her sides. They wear identical plain blue cotton outfits and white headbands with different characters on them: "Cook or Die" for the sous chef and "Eat or Die" for the kitchen assistant.

A bubble with large red characters flashes on the screen.

Level 4: Long-Life Noodles

I scan the ingredients on the bamboo shelves: rice noodles,

meat, oil, ginger, garlic, green onions, and an array of spices. It seems like we've made noodles a thousand times. Each time, something new goes wrong: the noodles are overcooked, the meat is bland, the sauce is too salty. So we've been stuck on level four for months as we have only passed six out of the ten recipes.

"Not noodles again!" groans Hong.

"Come on. Timer is running," I urge.

"Don't worry," Hong scoffs. "Speed is my best friend."

"My grandma made stir-fried noodles for dinner," says Ming.

"Stop chitchatting! Ming, get the meat ready. Hong, soak the rice noodles in warm water."

The sous chef tosses a slab of beef on a cutting board and slides his knife through it horizontally, cutting the meat into thin slices, while the kitchen assistant dumps a bag of rice noodles into a large wooden bucket.

I furiously press Control + C and the space bar on my keyboard to direct my avatar. She heats up a cup of oil in the wok, then throws a large piece of ginger and cloves of garlic onto the wooden cutting board. Cleaver in hand, she smashes the ingredients into pieces and tosses them into the sizzling oil, sending plumes of smoke into the air.

Hungry soldiers trudge to the kitchen windows. The health bar above their heads drops from green to yellow. They are getting weak, as zombies have mauled a few soldiers on the city wall.

"Hurry, they're going to die if we don't feed them soon!" I shout. "Hong, where are the noodles?"

"Uh-oh," Hong mumbles.

"What's wrong?" I scan the screen. The kitchen helper is scooping noodles from the sink.

"I spilled them when I dumped the water . . ."

"Beef is ready!" Ming cuts in.

The garlic and ginger are caramelizing in the sizzling oil.

"Okay, put the meat in, Ming!"

Suddenly, a violent cough echoes through my headset, and the sous chef stops moving.

"Ming!" I yell. "Hurry!"

"Sorry, my grandmother is sick. I have to go."

"Is she okay?" I ask, but the sous chef's avatar has already vanished.

The garlic and ginger turn black in the wok.

Zombies are eating your brains!
GAME OVER!

CHAPTER FIVE

人各有志

Each of us has our own ambitions and dreams

JANUARY 22, 2020, LATE MORNING

C-D-E-F-G-A-B-C...

    C-D-E-F-G...

Piano notes bounce above me. I pull a pillow over my head and try to drift back to sleep.

    C-D-E-F-G-A-B-C

    —CEGC...

I still haven't heard from Ming about Grandma, even though I sent him a few messages last night.

    Ding!

I snatch my phone, but it's just a WeChat message from Hong.

Hong:

Chef, can I please be the sous chef
for just one game today? 😇

Too tired to respond, I put down my phone and close my eyes
again. Maybe I should let Hong play the sous chef sometime.
After all, he did spend the coins he earned in single-player mode
to buy me a new spatula.

The piano continues. My life would be cheery if the *perfect*
girl upstairs didn't disrupt my sleep. Finally, I jump off the bed,
grab a broom from the kitchen, and rap the handle against the
ceiling. As if someone flipped a switch, the scales and chords
cease.

Since yesterday, school has closed down for Chinese New
Year. It's nice not having to worry about being late for class for
a few weeks. Now that Father is busier than usual, I have the
apartment all to myself to do what I please. But he doesn't totally
let me off the hook, texting a few times a day to check on me.
By now, I can almost predict what he's going to say depending
on the time of day.

12:00 PM:

Are you up yet? What are you doing?

33

3:00 PM:

Don't go outside. Have you done your quizzes?

6:00 PM:

What did you eat for dinner? Do you need
anything? Make sure you stay inside.

10:00 PM:

Don't stay up too late. Has Mrs.
Fong checked on you today?

Unlike my classmates, who spend all their free time at tutoring sessions and test-prep courses, I'm lucky to not have to attend any. When Mother's friends advised her to sign me up for the courses their children were enrolled in, she would shrug and say, "Mei is already taking piano classes. She has enough on her plate. I want her to have a childhood."

At the beginning of this school year, Father and I agreed on no extra prep courses, but I have to do two sets of questions every week from a fat green book, *Advanced Practice Quizzes*. He bought it online after the head nurse in his department raved about how it got her son into a good high school. It has two sections — math and English. I hate algebra but enjoy the folktale stories. My favorite is "Little Red Riding Hood," though I wonder how a wolf could just "gobble up" a grandma whole.

But lately, Father seems more concerned about me staying inside than the quizzes. He has never asked Mrs. Fong to check on me before. So far, I've managed to keep her at bay. When she came last night, I turned on the shower and waited. She set a new record—knocking eight times before giving up. Later, she even sent me a few WeChat messages.

Ding!

A text comes in.

Father:
Are you up yet? What are you doing?

Mei:
Yes, Dad! I was about to cook something to eat and then work on my math problems. How are you?

I walk into the kitchen.

Father:
Good. Do you need anything?

Mei:
No. I'm good.

I open the refrigerator and look at the stuffed shelves. I have everything I need to make lettuce cups.

Father:
Okay. Talk later.

Mei:
Wait! Ming's grandma is sick. Can you help?

Maybe he can get Grandma in, sparing her from waiting in the long line. When Father doesn't respond, I kick myself for not asking him right away. It will probably be hours before he checks his phone again.

The piano starts again, interrupting my thoughts. I can picture Piano Girl in her gray cashmere sweater, eyes half-closed as her slender, manicured fingers dance across her piano keys. How does she manage to stay perfectly on beat, nailing the triplet rhythm that always threw me off?

I reach into the back of the bottom cabinet, grab a handful of dried shiitake mushrooms from a ceramic jar, and drop them in a bowl of warm water. Mother said their rich, buttery flavor is what makes her lettuce cups special.

I started taking piano lessons when I was eight—a few years late by many of my parents' friends' standards. My teacher was a retired music professor, an old man who had enough wrinkles for three faces. His breath reeked of garlic, cigarettes, and black tea. Whenever he opened his mouth to speak, it reminded me of rotten vegetables.

"Flat fingers! Flat fingers!" He would raise his voice and tap my fingers with a small bamboo stick. I would quickly arch my fingers and then land on the wrong keys. I got so bored when he went on and on about augmented and diminished chords that I'd start counting the horn blasts on the Yangtze River outside his windows. The sound reminded me of the urgent cow horn in a Kung Fu game I played, warning the martial artists that enemies were near. My thoughts would jump from piano notes to my computer game. At the end of the class, my teacher would eye me with disapproval and wag his yellow, cigarette-stained fingers. In his heavy southern accent, he would say, "Practice, practice! You need to practice more. My good students practice at least an hour a day."

I rinse the mushrooms under running water and squeeze the liquid out of the caps before cutting them into small cubes.

I had many arguments with my parents about practice. I told them that if I spent an hour a day practicing cooking, I could have delicious food to eat. If I spent an hour playing my computer game, I could improve my scores. But when I spent an hour practicing piano, I only felt like a losing horse running a hopeless race.

I take the shrimp that I marinated last night out of the

refrigerator. The minute I open the glass container, the tangy and nutty smell of rice vinegar, soy sauce, and sesame oil seeps into the room. With each breath, my irritation at being woken up fades away.

Two years ago, when we first moved into this apartment, Piano Girl practiced every day. One night, Aunty was over for dinner when Piano Girl started playing the second movement of *The Yellow River*, a heroic concerto that exhibits the fighting spirit of the Chinese people. Father nodded to the beat with his eyes half-closed as Piano Girl transitioned effortlessly from a flowing traditional ode to a wild, wrathful movement before finally reaching the grandiose finale.

When she finished, he turned to me and said, "Mei, that is a beautiful piece. If you can play like her, we can duet with my erhu—"

"But I don't like playing piano," I interrupted. "And I don't want to be like her!"

Shouldn't he have known by then that I had no interest in playing piano? It annoyed me that he still dropped hints about it. I hated Piano Girl before I'd even met her.

"You should spend more time playing piano and less time on computer games . . ." Father continued.

"Stop!" Aunty raised her long, slender fingers with nicely painted red nails in front of him. "Let Mei walk her own path! Don't make her become someone else."

I looked at her with gratitude. Aunty always used her words like a sharp knife to cut off the rotten parts of a conversation. And she always stood up for me.

After that, whenever my parents pressured me to practice longer than thirty minutes a day, I would hold up my not-too-beautiful hand with short, plump fingers and say, "No! Let me walk my own path." I never got past playing the first movement of *The Yellow River.*

I lug out a head of iceberg lettuce and rinse it under the faucet while Piano Girl waltzes effortlessly through the adagio sostenuto of *Moonlight Sonata.* I hum along to the tune as I cut off the core from the leaves and then carefully separate them. Using scissors, I trim the leaves into eight perfect cups and place them onto a tray.

Moving around the kitchen, I step to the perfect staccato of the second movement — the allegretto. As carrots and apples turn into small unified cubes under my knife, I wonder if the girl upstairs finds playing piano as rewarding as I do cooking?

Even if I continued with my piano lessons, could I ever play like her? My teacher said I lacked passion. Do I have to fall in love with piano to play it well? Does her teacher also have stinky breath? If so, does she hold her breath like I did?

After Mother's death, I stopped my piano lessons. Father didn't bring them up. I wasn't sure if he was too busy to take me to class, or if he knew in his heart that it was a waste of time and money. It was one less thing we had to disagree about.

When the oil is heated in the wok, I toss in all the ingredients. Soon a plume of rich flavor rises in the air. The narrator in *Chop Chop* says that a good chef can judge a dish by its smell. Do I have a sharper sense of smell than others? If so, will it make me a naturally good chef? Are we born with talents?

It takes only a few minutes to stir-fry the shrimp and vegetables. I drizzle in some soy sauce and sesame oil and stir in pine nuts and green onions, then turn off the heat. Using a spoon, I scoop the mixture into the lettuce cups. I take my time carving a carrot into flower petals and place one in the middle of each cup. Proud, I snap a photo and send it to the Phoenix Group.

EmpressMei:
Look at my creation! 😌 😄

Hong sends me a thumbs-up. But Ming still doesn't respond. What's happening to Grandma? I take out my phone and call him again, but he doesn't pick up. Why has Father not gotten back to me? How long does he have to stay at the hospital? Will he be safe from this virus?

I place half the lettuce cups on a plate, wrap cling film over it, and put it in the refrigerator. The cups will taste even better after the flavors have a chance to blend, but I'm too hungry to wait. I sit down and eat the remaining ones.

The irritatingly bright tune of "The Entertainer" drifts down from upstairs. Suddenly, a painful memory flashes in my mind. It was the piece I played at my last recital. That day, I put on a red silk dress with black lace stitched into the collar, which Mother had bought me just for the occasion. I let my hair out of its usual ponytail. At the beginning of the recital, I played so beautifully that I remember thinking I had a hidden piano prodigy inside me after all.

When the photographer got on stage, I immediately straightened my spine, curved my fingers into a perfect ninety-degree angle, and forced a smile. When his camera shuttered and flashed, I struck the first wrong note. A chill trickled down my back. I tried to recover, but my fingers stiffened up and hit more wrong notes. Yet my hands didn't want to stop. I kept thinking I could get back on track, like harnessing a wild horse back to its racing lane. But the horse kept running in the wrong direction. Despite trying over and over, I could no longer syncopate my melody. I don't think my parents even bought the photograph, and we never talked about the recital.

"Food, food, Chinese food! Wok,
wok, iron wok. Stir, stir, stir-fry!"

"Wok," the hit song from my favorite rap band, Hungry Panda, blasts from my phone. I recently set it as my ringtone.
"Hello?"

"Mei!" Ming shouts. "I need your help."

"How is Grandma doing?" My heart thumps in my chest.

"She's getting worse, but we can't find a hospital willing to take her."

"I'll call my father. Tell me what's wrong with her."

"She has a fever and is coughing and struggling to breathe." Ming's voice trembles.

"Don't worry. I am sure my father can help. I'll get right back to you after I talk to him."

I call Father, but it goes straight to voicemail. I send him a text and wait for a few minutes, then call again. I can't remember ever calling him this many times in a month, let alone in one day.

Has Ming's grandmother contracted this new virus? Should I go to Father despite his order to stay away from the hospital?

If only I could call Aunty. She knows so many people and her pharmacy works with lots of doctors—but she probably won't pick up. Will she ever get over my choice to live with Father instead of her? I stumble around the apartment from room to room, feeling like a soldier in *Chop Chop,* trapped in the walled city.

Finally, I grab the plate of lettuce cups from the refrigerator, put on a mask, and step out into the cold, crowded streets.

SHRIMP AND VEGETABLES IN LETTUCE CUPS

Makes 24 lettuce cups

HERE'S WHAT YOU NEED:

4 medium heads Boston or butter lettuce

¼ cup cooking oil

2 teaspoons peeled and minced fresh ginger

2 cloves garlic, minced

8 ounces fresh baby shrimp

½ cup finely cubed baby carrot

½ cup finely cubed green apple

2 tablespoons soy sauce

1 teaspoon sesame oil

½ cup pine nuts

2 green onions, minced

HERE'S WHAT YOU DO:

Cut out the lettuce core and separate the leaves. Rinse leaves and pat dry. Be careful not to tear them. Arrange the "cups" on a large serving plate.

Heat cooking oil in a medium nonstick skillet over medium heat and swirl to coat. Add ginger and garlic. Stir-fry until fragrant, about 30 seconds. Add shrimp and stir-fry for 2 minutes. Add carrot and apple and stir-fry for 30 seconds.

Add soy sauce. Cook, stirring occasionally, until vegetables are heated through, about 2 minutes. Stir in sesame oil, pine nuts, and green onions. To serve, spoon 2 tablespoons of the mixture into the center of each lettuce leaf cup, wrap, and eat with your hands.

CHAPTER SIX

飞蛾投火

A moth flies toward a flame, despite the danger

JANUARY 22, 2020, EARLY AFTERNOON

Storm clouds brew over the setting sun. Countless cars clog the streets, spill onto sidewalks, and block the crosswalks. Impatient drivers honk horns and roll down their windows to curse at pedestrians and halted cars. I wait on the edge of the sidewalk until I see a small gap between two cars and start to make my way across the street.

I inch near the front of a black sedan and peek into the windshield. I hesitate for a moment when I see the eyes of the driver — a woman with short, permed hair — are staring off into space, somewhere far in the distance. Scanning the traffic-jammed street, I make sure she has nowhere to move before running across.

When I was in first grade, Mother taught me how to cross a busy road: make eye contact with the driver and walk with determination. Did she forget to do that on that dreadful day? Or did she not see the car coming?

As I walk past the line of patients bundled in heavy winter coats, a few muster the energy to lift their heads and look at me with dull eyes. They hide their faces behind scarfs or masks.

Standing at the back of the line, an old man in a down jacket wraps a scarf around his mouth as a makeshift mask. His neck juts forward as if it takes too much effort to hold it up, and his back hunches like a round hill. Suddenly, he breaks into a coughing fit and doubles over. I hurry away.

Yangtze Hospital is one of the most famous hospitals in the city, known for its respiratory care department. Its three buildings stretch over half a block like a phoenix spreading its wings, shielding the neighborhood. Father's department is at the top floor of the middle building. Once, when a newspaper came to interview him, I heard Father tell the reporter that they were always busy because the hospital is located in the middle of the dense residential area. I thought he should've also told the reporter it's because they are always featured in the news and have a big online fan page.

I've never seen this many patients packed in the lobby. A strong disinfectant smell permeates the air, piercing through my mask. The fluorescent light casts a yellow glow over the patients, who occupy every row of the bright green padded seats. They are bundled in thick coats and a few have cloth masks on. Those who can't get a seat slouch against the walls. Stuck in the middle of the crowd, I slowly push my way across the room.

"Move, move. Please! Let me through!"

A short nurse with glasses lifts an IV bag over her head with one hand while she navigates through the huddled bodies, parting a way for herself. All eyes follow her. As soon as she passes, the crowd quickly seals back like a thin stew.

A young couple wearing matching red brocade jackets adorned with yellow dragons squeeze past me. I remember that Chinese New Year is just a couple of days away.

"Look!" says the man. "Even the nurse doesn't have a mask on! Didn't I tell you the city officials said the virus doesn't transmit from human to human?"

"How can you believe that? Look around—" The woman's voice is interrupted by her violent coughs. Her chin-length black hair falls across her pale face. People around shoot her angry looks.

"You should have brought your mask," says the man, wrapping his arm around her shoulders to keep her steady.

The crowd stops moving for a moment. The nurse has made her way to a metal pole that stands between rows of chairs. On wobbly tiptoes, and with shaking hands, she hangs the IV bag on the rusted pole next to a slouching old man whose eyes are closed.

"Excuse me, young lady!" An elderly woman grips the nurse's arm. Her white hair is coiled back into a bun, like Ming's grandma.

The nurse pulls away from the old lady and shouts, as if she wants to make sure everyone in the lobby hears her, "Don't grab me! Can't you see I'm busy?"

The old lady takes a step back and almost trips on a man's walker. Once she regains her balance, her face twists in anger and she cries out, "Young lady, do you know who my son is? He works at—"

The nurse's thin eyebrows shoot up. "I am sure your son is very important. But with all due respect, you still have to wait for your turn."

I look at the nurse's fierce eyes with respect. Like Aunty, she is good at cutting out the rotten parts of a conversation. But why isn't she wearing a mask? Maybe the virus isn't as contagious as Father said.

"I have been waiting for hours! I need he . . . hel . . ." The old lady breaks into a cough and then wheezes like a leaky balloon. The nurse leans forward and gently pats the old lady's back.

I fight my way through the lobby, hugging the plate closer to my chest. People push and shove around me. I shuffle my feet close to the floor, knowing if I lift them, I will have nowhere to put them down.

I finally make it into the elevator, ducking my face under my jacket collar for extra protection from the coughing around me. I dart my eyes around at the people and see panic and fear on their faces.

The elevator stops at every floor and more wheezing people squeeze in. I regret not taking the stairs. Pinned against the wall, I take short breaths, the edge of the plate digging into my side. I glance down at the lettuce cups, now shriveled and wilted. Why didn't I think of putting them in a sealed Tupperware? Do coughs contaminate food? The thought makes me queasy.

DING!

At last, the doors slide open on the fifth floor, and everyone surges into the packed corridor of the respiratory care department. A nurse in a white uniform floats in the sea of patients. She manages to climb onto a chair at the end of the hallway and shout at the crowd through a megaphone.

"Please leave your forms here and go wait in the lobby on the first floor! We will call your name when it's your turn."

"I'm not going anywhere," a young man shouts. "My father and I have been waiting in line since early morning!"

Others murmur in agreement.

"We are shorthanded. We can't do our work with you all gathered here!"

Cursing loudly, the crowd barges forward, then comes to a complete stop. I peek through the crack of an ajar door. In a ward the size of a classroom, beds are lined up against the wall. On one bed, a doctor is securing a clear oxygen mask over a patient's face. A blue plastic tube connects the mask to a white beeping machine.

At another bed, two nurses lift a motionless man onto a stretcher while a third nurse helps a new patient climb into the bed. Aren't they supposed to change the sheets between patients?

I inch forward to get a better look at the man on the stretcher. Mouth open, he stares blankly at the ceiling. His pale skin is almost translucent. A nurse drapes an orange sheet over his entire body. My heart thunders in my chest.

"Hey, move, move!" a gruff male voice shouts.

Startled, my foot trips on something sharp, shooting a stinging pain up my thigh.

"Watch where you're going, young lady!"

Like a ballerina making a bad turn, I wobble and fall onto my side. The plate hits the floor and sends lettuce, shrimp, carrots, and scallions in every direction. Heart hammering, I push myself up on my arms.

"Are you okay?" asks the same gruff voice. I look up at a plump person covered from head to toe in a white hazmat suit.

I nod, and the man steers the metal cart around me and hurries on. One shrimp is flattened under the wheels of his rolling cart, which holds a respirator machine. Still in shock, I fight to hold back tears and am struggling to stand up when a strong hand lifts me off the ground. I glance at a tall person in the same type of hazmat suit.

Without saying anything, he pulls me through the room. We

walk past the beds, each holding a patient covered with white sheets, only their faces exposed. He stops in front of a door and presses a keycard against a scanner. *Click!* The door opens.

He pushes me inside and the door closes behind me. I wiggle the handle—it's locked. The air is stale with the smell of a strange mixture of disinfectant and beef noodle soup. It takes my eyes a moment to adjust to the poorly lit room, as the only source of light comes from a small square window above a wooden desk.

A single bed is set against the left wall. Draped over the edge is a heavy white comforter with YANGTZE HOSPITAL printed on it. Across from the bed stands a glass cabinet filled with bottles, powders, and pills, labelled with neat white stickers and tidy black handwriting.

My breath quickens. Who is this person? What is this room for? Am I in trouble? I move to the desk and examine the clutter that covers every inch of its top: prescription notes, a half-empty box of surgical gloves, a stack of medical journals, and an open carton of Kang Shi Fu Roasted Beef instant noodles. I pull out my phone and am about to call Father when I see a familiar photo in a picture frame behind a stack of patient charts. The door opens, and the person returns, holding a blue mask sealed in a plastic bag.

"Mei, put this on!" He takes out the mask shaped like a turtle shell.

I recognize the voice immediately.

"F-Father!"

Father removes the hood of his suit. He is wearing a mask identical to the one he is holding.

"Why did you come here?"

"I brought you some food, but I spilled it," I say in a choked voice.

"Didn't I tell you to stay away from the hospital?" He removes the thin mask from my face, carefully folds it inside out, and throws it in a trash can behind the door.

"Yes, but I haven't seen you for days." I immediately regret my words. I must sound like a needy little kid. I quickly add, "My friend's grandma is sick. Can you help her?"

Father acts as if he doesn't hear me. He puts on a pair of blue disposable gloves and then places the blue mask over my face by hooking the top and bottom straps behind my head. The edge of the mask digs into my face, and I find it hard to breathe through it.

"This N95 mask will give you better protection, but still, don't come here again."

"Why? The nurse downstairs is not even wearing a mask." I'm annoyed he didn't answer my question about helping Ming's grandma.

Father sighs. "That's because they believe what the city officials are saying. I'm afraid they'll soon find out the truth."

I look at Father's bloodshot eyes behind his clear, horn-rimmed glasses. His hair has grown shaggy and gray. In just a few days, he has changed so much.

"I told you not to come to the hospital unless it's an emergency. Why are you here?" Did he forget he asked me this question before?

"I . . . I made . . ." Against my will, tears well up in my eyes. "Shrimp . . . lettuce cups . . . for you."

"Mei—"

"B-but . . . but they're all ruined!" I avoid his gaze, take a few steps back, and stare at our family photo on the desk. People say I inherited Mother's big dimples and slim build, and Father's double eyelids and wide shoulders.

"Mei . . ." Father moves closer to me. "Thank you for bringing me food."

"But it's ruined," I mutter.

"I'm sure they would've tasted delicious, because you made them." His eyes squint into a smile.

"Now, tell me what's wrong with your friend's grandmother."

"She has a fever, cough, and trouble breathing," I say quickly.

Father's eyebrows knit together, deepening the wrinkles on his forehead.

"Can you please help her?"

"I am sorry. There is really nothing I can do at the moment.

She is better off staying at home than coming here and risking getting infected."

"Couldn't you just slip her in?"

In the past, whenever our relatives or neighbors were sick, Mother always managed to get them help right away.

"Not now, Mei! We don't even have beds for our doctors and nurses." Father opens the glass cabinet and takes out a plastic prescription bottle with a bright yellow cap. "I was saving these for emergencies, and I suppose this counts as one. The instructions are on the bottle. Make sure you wear the N95 mask when you meet with your friend."

"Thanks!" I take the bottle from him and stuff it in my pocket. Eager to get the medicine to Grandma, I dash to the door.

"Wait!" Father reaches into his desk drawer and takes out another turtle-shell mask. "This mask is very hard to come by now. Take good care of it! You can reuse it after airing it outside. Rotate it every two days with the one you have on. It's very important that you wash your hands with soap before and after you handle it."

I nod and put it in my pocket. Father leads me to the back stairs. Just when I am about to bolt down the steps, he grabs my arm, looks around, and pulls me closer to him.

"Mei, this is a new, very contagious virus," he whispers. "Don't believe anything else you hear."

CHAPTER SEVEN

患难见真情

In hardship we see true friendship

JANUARY 22, 2020, MIDAFTERNOON

Once outside the hospital, I send Ming another message.

> **Mei:**
> Hey, answer me! I have medicine for Grandma.

Last time I went to his house, I took the no. 6 bus for one stop. But today the streets are packed with people with no buses in sight. I start walking down Victory Road. I wish Ming would get back to me soon, as I'm not sure if I can get past the guards at his gate by myself.

A month ago, Ming invited me over to play *Chop Chop*. Even though his home was only a twenty-minute walk from mine, it might as well have been a different world. At the big iron gate in front of his apartment complex, two middle-aged guards in blue uniforms stopped me. One asked me for my ID in a heavy northern accent. The shorter one handed me a form. Beside my name, I had to fill out my age, address, and purpose of visit. I wasn't sure if they would let me in if I put down "playing *Chop Chop*." Thankfully, Ming showed up.

Inside the gate, Ming and I walked along a paved path lined with trees and nicely trimmed shrubs that led to their apartment. His home is located on the first floor of the three-story building. Across from their front lawn is a pond with a fountain shaped like a lotus flower, with water spraying out in all directions.

His grandma, a soft-spoken old lady with gray hair neatly pinned back in a bun, greeted me warmly at the door.

"Welcome. Let me take your coat. And you can wear these." She took out a pair of green slippers from a well-organized shoe rack next to the door and placed them in front of me. When she stood up, her small reading glasses attached to a colorful beaded chain swung around her neck.

I blushed at the thought of our messy entranceway, with shoes all over and coats crowded on top of the three hooks. I nervously gave her my coat and wished I had wiped my boots on the floor mat outside the door.

Their apartment was different from any home I have visited. It had fewer walls and a much higher ceiling than ours.

Everything seemed to be put in its proper place. Ming led me to a steel dining room table that faced a big window. The silver, curved lines etched across it reminded me of twirling dragon tails. Sunlight filtered through the glossy osmanthus leaves outside. In the middle of the table stood a short glass vase holding an elegant floral arrangement. Colorful blossoms nested at the center of thin branches that curved upward, as if to hug the ceiling. The flowers must have come from somewhere much warmer than Wuhan.

At first, I felt uneasy in such a fancy place. After learning his parents were not home, I became less anxious. Ming told me his parents worked at a US–China joint-venture company.

Grandma brought us two small plates filled with sesame candies, rice crackers, and candied winter melon.

"Try some! I made these." As she put the plate down, a sweet fragrance of magnolia wafted over from her.

"Thank you, Grandma." I gave her my most polite smile.

Ming launched the game. Large red characters flashed across the screen.

Level 4: Scallion Pancakes

We quickly move our avatars in position. When I directed my avatar to dump a bucket of water into the flour, white powder exploded, turning our avatars white as ghosts. The dough looked like soup. "I think we messed up," Ming said in a small voice.

"What happened?" Ming's grandma came over with her glasses perched on her nose. "Would you like some tips on making dough?"

I quickly stood up to offer her my chair, as I was taught to do when around elders. Grandma patted my shoulder and sat down.

She looked at us and said keenly, "It's very crucial to mix in the water a little at a time, because the amount of water you need varies depending on the weather, temperature, and type of flour you use."

Since then, Ming and I have been wanting to try making scallion pancakes again, but the recipe hasn't been shuffled back to us.

For the third time, I run my fingers over the zipper of my pocket to make sure the medicine bottle is secure inside. The setting sun looks like a huge rice cake sliced in half by the tall TV tower in the distance. The few well-stocked grocery stores on the way to Ming's apartment are strangely quiet, with only one or two masked customers inside.

A small store across the street catches my attention. It has a wooden stand outside filled with bags of nuts, chilies, wood ear and dried shiitake mushrooms. I think of the shrimp in the refrigerator. If I can get some peanuts, I can make kung pao shrimp. I decide after I deliver the medicine to Grandma, I will stop by to pick up a few ingredients.

I pause half a block away and call Ming, hoping he will come out and spare me from having to fill out the guest form. Still no answer. If I can't get past the guards, I'll leave the medicine at the gate, but I really want to see Grandma.

I'm halfway across the street when a large white van streaks past me. It stops in front of the iron gate of Ming's apartment complex. I hurry toward it. Two men in white hazmat suits carry a stretcher out of the gate, a group of people following behind. My heart races when I see Ming, walking alongside the stretcher. Next to him is a woman who has his same pale, smooth skin. Close behind them is a tall, Western-looking man with light brown curly hair. They all wear identical blue surgical masks. A knot forms in my stomach. Grandma!

I run toward them, but they have already climbed into the van. The door closes and the ambulance zips away. Pain stings my heart. Why do bad things happen to nice people like Mother and Grandma?

Palms sweating, I call Ming again but he doesn't pick up. I then send him a WeChat message and a text, but still no response. Disheartened, I cross the street to make my way home when a flashing ambulance races past me, sirens blaring. Its force flips up my ponytail. I turn to get a better look at it and bump into a bald man who has stuffed shopping bags slung on his neck, shoulders, and arms. How many people is he shopping for?

My thoughts darken again as I think of Grandma. Are they taking her to a hospital or . . . I don't want to finish my thought. The idea of going back to the empty apartment saddens me. There has to be something I can do to help.

"Food, food, Chinese food! Wok,
wok, iron wok. Stir, stir, stir-fry!"

I answer quickly.

"Little Apple, how are you?" a raspy voice booms.

I stop in my tracks. "Aunty!"

Aunty gave me the nickname Little Apple because she says I had chubby, red cheeks when I was little.

My throat tightens with emotion. I haven't heard her voice in so long. I can't believe she is calling me now.

"Where are you, Mei?"

"I'm walking home."

"You shouldn't be out right now." She sounds worried. "Where's your father?"

Like always, Aunty doesn't give me a chance to respond and answers her own question.

"I bet he is at work, huh! I doubt you've seen that man for days."

I want to defend Father, but I'm afraid to say something that will upset her.

"Listen, Mei, this virus is very dangerous. Wait for me at home. I will be there tomorrow at noon."

"Aunty . . ." Aunty has already hung up.

CHAPTER EIGHT

热锅上的蚂蚁，坐立不安

Jumping like ants in a hot wok

JANUARY 23, 2020, EARLY MORNING

Bzzzz! Bzzzz! Bzzzz!

My body lurches forward. Are ambulances coming? I open my eyes. Outside, it's still dark and gloomy. The wind roars and raindrops pitter-patter on the balcony. Pellets hit the window ledge and strike the panes.

I was dreaming of ambulances charging into our courtyard.

Bzzzz! Bzzzz! Bzzzz!

I feel around my nightstand until my hand lands on my fried egg alarm clock, a gift from Aunty.

Bzzzz! Bzzzz! Bzzzz!

I press the snooze button in the middle, but the buzzing sound continues. It's coming from my phone. Is Ming finally calling me back? I squint at the blinding screen to let my eyes adjust to its brightness. It's not a call. It's an . . . alert?

Public Safety Alert!

In response to the outbreak of the new coronavirus, Wuhan Municipal Epidemic Prevention and
Control Headquarters has officially decided to close
the city. At 10:00 AM, the city will suspend its buses,
subways, ferries, and all long-distance transportation systems. At 2:00 PM, all highways, airports, and
railway stations will be temporarily closed. Unless
under special circumstances, nobody will be allowed
to travel in or out of Wuhan.

All schools, offices, and shops will be closed. All
residents should stay at home. Masks are required
for going outside, and spitting is prohibited.

The Center for Disease Control and Prevention

I rub my groggy eyes and read it again. What does "close the city" mean? How many people have gotten the virus? Do all those patients in Father's hospital have it? Is that why he hasn't been able to come home? Will a mask and hazmat suit be enough to protect him? I slip back underneath the warm comforter and text Father.

Mei:

Dad, did you see the alert? When are
you coming home? I'm worried.

I read the alert a third time. How long are they going to shut down the city? Father always says Wuhan, as the capital of the province, is like a human heart—all the blood travels through it. If the heart stops, what will happen to the rest of the Hubei province? How I wish Mother were here to answer my questions. Should I call Aunty? She would know what to do. I look at the time on my phone—2:02 AM.

I sigh. Aunty hates being woken up, and besides, she silences her phone at night. There's nothing I can do now. I just have to wait for her to come tomorrow.

I wake up to a blast of car horns, shouting, doors slamming, and suitcase wheels rolling. I jump out of bed and run to the window. People rush in and out of the buildings that surround the courtyard, dragging suitcases and large bags with them. A torn red Chinese New Year couplet dances in the wind along with yellow hand-shaped leaves. A plastic take-out bag with a Double Happy logo flaps on a branch of the camphor tree next to the playground.

Thoughts race through my mind. Why hasn't Father gotten back to me? I send him another text. Will Aunty still be able to come today? She and Mother always had their ways of putting me at ease—Mother by listening and comforting me, Aunty by giving me a solution. I need to tidy up the apartment. Aunty hates mess. Maybe I should cook something for her. That always makes her happy.

CRASH!

My head jerks upward. It sounds like something shattered upstairs. A woman's screams and a man's shouts echo loudly.

BANG!

A door slams shut.

All is quiet and then—a woman sobs. Is Piano Girl fighting with her parents? It can't be. Whenever we pass each other on the stairs, she looks so perfect and composed that I avoid making eye contact with her. It has to be her parents arguing. Maybe her life isn't so sunny after all. The thought oddly pleases me, but guilt quickly sets in. She has never done anything to hurt me besides being *perfect*. The sobbing upstairs stops and all is quiet again.

I go to the kitchen and plan what to cook for Aunty. The safety alert says to stay home, which is fine by me, so long as I have food and can play *Chop Chop*. I remember the packet of calcium sulfate I bought a while ago to make tofu out of soy milk. I bet she will be impressed that I can make tofu from scratch. I open the refrigerator and pull out the carton of soy milk, but it's almost empty.

I decide to run to the neighborhood store near Double Happy, even though it's more expensive than the big grocery stores. Hopefully Mrs. Fong won't see me and tell Father.

I slip my down jacket on, put on my N95 mask, and dash out the door. As I walk through the courtyard, I look at all the closed windows and empty balconies, wondering how many people are fighting like Piano Girl's parents.

A big mushroom cloud hangs over the hospital as if it might swallow the buildings at any moment. The rain has stopped. I carefully step over puddles gathered in the lower depths of the street. Overnight, the city has transformed into a different world. Men in green uniforms and red armbands direct cars, bicycles, and people who are weighed down by heavy bags and suitcases. The large buses that usually dominate the middle of the street are absent. Has the government already suspended them? Are all these people trying to get out before the city closes down? If Mother were here, would we also try to leave? But where would we go? I bet Mother would have had a plan.

I push my way through the sea of people blocking the sidewalk outside the stores. People rush around in homemade face and body coverings. One woman has tied an orange peel around her face with shoelaces. The man next to her wears a plastic water gallon jug over his head like a scuba diving helmet. The strangest masks are the ones made from underwear, bras, and Halloween masks.

I feel safe with my N95 mask, even though it's harder to breathe through than those paper-thin ones. I should ask Father if wearing a fruit peel will give me the same protection. If so, I will make one with my favorite fruit, watermelon.

As shocked and nervous as I am, I break out in laughter when I walk by a man who has covered his body with a trash bag and his head with cabbage leaves. He cut two holes for his eyes and one for his mouth, from which a long cigarette sticks out.

I pause to watch two women walk side by side under a large plastic tablecloth draped over an umbrella. They muscle their way through a small bakery door but are pushed out by an old man wearing a mask made from a pink sanitary napkin, juggling armloads of bags out of the store.

Outside Double Happy, Executive Chef Ma is bowing over a big, round table that blocks the sidewalk. It's piled high with cooking utensils, spices, and bags of noodles. I walk around it and see he is wrapping a familiar-looking blue clay pot with sheets of newspaper. I muster up some cheeriness and greet him.

"Hello, Chef Ma."

He looks up and stares at me blankly.

A mask made of half a green grapefruit peel is secured around his protruding ears with shoelaces. Does the peel smell as sour as the fruit tastes?

"It's me, Mei Li, Dr. Wong's daughter." Does he not remember me? I feel embarrassed.

"Oh, hello, Mei! Where are you going? Do you need any food? Here, take . . ."

He stops midsentence and turns to three young men who have identical lemon-peel masks on. Two of them are wheeling out trays of dumplings, scallion pancakes, deep-fried meatballs, tofu, and vegetables. The third one is pushing a portable stove.

"Dong, take the fresh produce to the school and put it in the refrigerator right away." His voice jumps a few octaves. "Tao, leave the stove here. We will move them with the table when the truck gets here."

He turns back toward me and tilts his chin at the line of people waiting outside the grocery store across the street.

"It may be hard to get food for a while." He sets the pot down and grabs a bag of scallion pancakes from the table and thrusts it at me. "Take this!"

"No thank you!" I take a step back. "We have a lot of food at home. Are you moving?"

"Not exactly. The city is shutting down all restaurants. We are temporarily moving to Yangtze Middle School." His eyes squeeze into two triangles and he points in the direction of the market. "We are setting up an emergency kitchen to cook for frontline medical workers."

"Oh, that's my school!" I say excitedly. "Can I join you? I can cook . . ."

Chef Ma pulls me aside to make room for a truck pulling up next to us.

"Hurry! It's illegal for me to park here," a man shouts, sticking his head out from the driver's side. "I don't want to get another ticket!" He pushes up his mask—made from half a black lace bra—and rests his arm on the windowsill.

Chef Ma calls out toward the restaurant, "Everyone, come out to help!"

Someone yells back from inside the restaurant. Chef Ma mutters something under his breath and says to me, "Please take some food. I've got to go!" He hurries inside.

"I am fine. Thank you!" I call after him and continue walking.

I recall the unforgettable dish he cooked for us in that clay pot. About two years ago, one night after dinner, he came to our home with a fancy gift bag. He said to Mother, "I took my daughter to so many doctors and spent most of my savings, but no one could help her except you!"

"I'm glad I could help, but I can't accept your gift," Mother said softly.

"Oh, please accept our gratitude!" Beads of sweat broke out on his forehead.

I was surprised that such a short and skinny person could talk so loudly. He sounded like he was about to cry. Father came out from his study holding a medical journal and said, "She is just doing her job. The best reward for our doctors is healing patients."

I felt sorry for Chef Ma and wished they would make an exception and accept his gift. In the end, Mother made him keep the gift, but agreed to go to Double Happy to taste some of his signature dishes.

The following weekend, we went to the restaurant. Chef Ma came out and greeted us warmly, setting a big clay pot in the middle of the table. Two waiters followed closely behind him, each carrying a big tray loaded with local delicacies. I took in each dish as they placed them before us.

Doupi — sticky rice cooked with roasted beef, dry mushrooms, and pickled vegetables wrapped in a soft skin made of a mixture of green bean powder, flour, and eggs, then pan-fried to crispy golden; steamed Wuchang fish — a local fish steamed with ham, bamboo shoots, and mushrooms, garnished with shredded scallions and ginger; pearl meatballs — steamed meatballs coated with sticky rice; dry-cooked string beans stir-fried with garlic and minced pork. The other diners shot us envious looks.

Finally, Chef Ma removed the cover of the clay pot. The soup was still bubbling and a flowery aroma rose up like a hot spring. I picked up a small piece of lotus root. It tasted tender and starchy, bursting with flavor.

"So good, try it, Mom!" I put a piece into Mother's bowl.

Mother and I loved the lotus root rib soup so much, we even bought a clay pot to make it ourselves, but ours tasted nothing like Chef Ma's. After Mother's death, that dinner frequently appeared in my dreams.

"Watch it, kid!"

My thoughts are interrupted by a woman wearing a large plastic water jug over her head. She almost runs me over with her bicycle. I mutter an apology and push my way through the busy street. Anxious customers cluster outside overcrowded stores while other shop owners are boarding their windows and doors.

Finally, I arrive at my destination. From outside the store, I hear a commotion.

CHAPTER NINE

见义勇为

Step forward bravely for what is right

JANUARY 23, 2020, LATE MORNING

There are only about a dozen people inside the store, but the shelves are mostly bare. A young woman is standing near a checkout counter, waving her arms up and down, yelling at a fragile-looking old woman wearing a homemade cloth mask. A few customers watch from a distance.

"Give me the bag!" the young woman shouts through her N95 mask.

"Please, I need it." The old woman speaks with the same soft voice as Ming's grandmother. She's hugging a bag of rice to her chest. "My son is very sick, and we have no more rice left."

"I had my eyes on it long before you did." The young woman takes a step forward and blocks the old woman from her empty shopping cart.

The panicked look on the old woman's face stirs something inside me. How can this young woman be so disrespectful to an elder? I dash forward and shove the cart away from her. It catches the young woman by surprise.

"Stop! Respect the *elderly*," I say firmly.

"Where did you come from, little hooligan?" the woman asks testily.

Ignoring her, I help the old woman load the bag of rice into her cart.

"Thank you!" says the old woman with teary eyes, stumbling away.

"Who do you think you are?" The young woman scowls and takes a step toward me. I meet her heavily lined eyes.

"I am nobody. What do you want?" I glare back at her.

"I want my rice!"

I size her up. She's taller than me, but scrawny. If she starts a fight, I have a chance of winning.

She steps closer to me. I notice her right eye looks bigger than her left one, like the zany face emoji. Did she run to the store before she had a chance to put eyeliner on both eyes? Suddenly, a middle-aged woman dressed in the store's blue uniform throws herself in between us. I notice her bloodshot eyes.

"Go! Go! We are closing. Everyone leave!" She points at the door.

"Could I just get a bottle of soy milk?" I ask.

"All the milk sold out hours ago." The clerk shoos us as if she is chasing away chickens from grain.

"Will you have some tomorrow?"

"No, young lady! Starting now, all shops will be closed down."

"Why couldn't you have given us more notice?" a short man asks, his face scrunched with anger.

"Don't yell at me, man! We were just notified this morning."

"What are we going to eat?" The man lifts up his empty shopping bag.

"Your neighborhood committee will take care of you," says a young clerk with a pixie cut, walking toward us.

"Yeah, I should believe that." He laughs mockingly. "Just like I should believe the city officials telling us that the disease is controllable and doesn't transmit human to human."

The young clerk walks over to calm the man down. I make my way toward the door and see the young woman kneeling in the corner, checking the bottom of an empty shelf.

Walking home, I replay what just happened. Did the young woman run out of food at home? Is she as scared as I am? But I have a kitchen full of food.

My phone dings. I ignore it until I enter the apartment, take off my shoes, hang the mask on a hook near the door, and wash my hands. It's a message from the neighborhood WeChat group.

Dear Neighbors,

I want to inform you that as of today, January 23, 2020, the central government of China has imposed a lockdown in Wuhan in an effort to quarantine the center of the coronavirus outbreak.

Travel restrictions are imposed and highway exits are closed. To control the outbreak and limit the number of people in public places, shops and restaurants are shut down. The neighborhood committee will deliver groceries to you.

Stay calm, stay inside, and stay safe! We will update you on any new developments through our WeChat group.

Sincerely,

Mrs. Fong Zhai

Director of Neighborhood Committee

If the stores are empty and closed, where will Mrs. Fong get food for thirty families? I'm glad Father stocked our kitchen, but I still need soy milk. Should I ask her to get it for me?

Bang! Bang! Bang!

"Little Apple, it's me!" a familiar raspy voice shouts. "Open up!"

CHAPTER TEN

人算不如天算

Life can interfere with one's plans

JANUARY 23, 2020, EARLY AFTERNOON

Heart pounding, I open the door. Aunty rushes in, bringing along the dewy scent of peony from her favorite moisturizer.

Her eyes scan me from head to toe.

"Are you okay?"

I open and close my mouth a few times but fail to make any sounds. I want to tell her that I'm okay physically, but I'm scared and sad. As usual, Aunty doesn't wait for me to answer. She kicks off her leather ankle boots and struts into the apartment, keeping her N95 mask on.

"How long has your father left you by yourself?" she calls out from the kitchen. "Do you have any food? What have you been eating?"

"Father's been gone for just a few days. But he bought me lots of food." I follow her into the kitchen, glad I cleared all the dirty dishes in the sink.

Aunty opens the refrigerator and surveys the different drawers. She has cut her hair to below her ears and changed her highlights from dark brown to caramel. A plaid shawl is wrapped over the collar of her white cinched-waist down jacket. Mother used to say that there was no need for her to buy new clothes; she could be the most fashionable doctor in the hospital just by wearing Aunty's hand-me-downs. But I hardly ever saw Mother wear anything Aunty gave her.

"Can I make you some tea, Aunty?"

"No, I can't stay long." She closes the refrigerator door. "Pack up your things."

"Where are we going?"

"To my place. You can't stay here by yourself."

As much as I love Aunty, the thought of living in her showroom-like home and following her strict rules makes me wince. Every time I visit, her apartment is sparkling clean. If I live there, I know I will have to make my bed every day, dry my cleaned dishes completely, and keep the kitchen as spotless as a laboratory. I don't think I can meet her high standards. Most important, I want to be here when Father comes home.

"Thanks, but Dad will be back soon. And he has Mrs. Fong checking on me every day."

Aunty narrows her eyes, giving me a familiar disapproving

look. A cold sweat breaks out on my back. The last time I refused to live with her, she didn't talk to me for over a year.

"Mei . . ."

"You are my little rice cake, like the
morning sun in the sky . . ."

A cheerful tune blasts from her Coach bag. Aunty zips open the purse and searches for her phone.

"Spring arrives again, and flowers
bloom all over the mountainside.
I reap the hopes that I sewed . . ."

Wow, Aunty chose "Morning Sun" by the popular rock band Chopsticks Brothers as her ringtone. I thought only teenagers liked them. But Aunty's tastes are always on trend.

"Hello! What do you mean you can't find the key?" Her eyebrows knit together. "Of course I have a spare one. I'll be there soon."

She drops her phone into her bag and pulls out a set of keys. "I have to go to the emergency kitchen now."

"The one at my school?"

"Yes—I am the director."

"Can I come?" I follow her to the door.

"No. I'm in a hurry." She slips on her boots.

"I know how to cook! I can help you there." There is still so much I want to tell her. I am terrified that she will disappear again from my life.

Aunty pauses and looks back at me, hand on the door handle.

"I will be right back," she says. "I haven't eaten anything all morning." Aunty pats her stomach and winks at me. When I was little, we used to play a game. She would rub her stomach and act as if she were hungry, and I would run to my toy kitchen to cook for her.

"I can cook you something!"

"I know you will!" Aunty gazes at me fondly and then bolts out.

"I'll have food waiting for you when you come back," I call after her.

She disappears as fast as she arrived, leaving only the lingering scent of peony. Ever since Mother died, I have dreamed of the moment Aunty would come back into my life. There were so many times I wanted to call her but feared she was still upset with me. I wish I could have found a way to decline her invitation without disappointing her again, but I can't abandon Father. More than once, I've caught him staring at Mother's photo in tears when he thought I wasn't looking.

I walk into the kitchen and look at the veggie clock hanging above the sink. Aunty gave it to me for my tenth birthday. I was so in love with it and spent a long time admiring the twelve vegetables dotting its circumference. I told her that someday I'd cook her a dish with all the vegetables in it. Now both of its arms—a carrot and a green onion—are pointed at the red bell pepper at the top. It's noon, which means I need to think of something exceptional but quick. A dish that impresses Aunty enough to post on her WeChat Moments, alongside all the fancy dishes she has eaten.

I open the refrigerator and survey the ingredients. I won't impress her with simple stir-fried rice or noodles with spicy sesame sauce. I spot the chicken breast on the bottom shelf and remember Auntie's favorite chicken curry dish from the restaurant Little Bangkok. In the last episode of *Cooking Delicious,* the chef with the caterpillar eyebrows demonstrated how to make Thai red curry.

He went on and on about his top cooking secret. In the end, it boiled down to using coconut cream instead of coconut milk. He could have saved everyone's time and said it in one sentence. I wondered if he kept babbling on so he could fill the half-hour show. The next day, I picked up a carton of coconut cream on my way home from school, and I've been wanting to make the curry dish ever since.

With my eight-inch chef's knife, it doesn't take me long to chop all the necessary ingredients, which I arrange in bowls like chefs do on cooking shows. I heat two spoonfuls of coconut oil in an iron pan and sauté onions, ginger, garlic, and red chilies. The warm scent fills the kitchen. I haven't felt this excited in a long time. I stir in cubed taro root and chicken, add two spoonfuls of red curry paste, and mix in coconut cream and water.

The sweet and pungent smell grows heavier as wisps of steam escape through the glass lid. It reminds me of the happy times I spent with Aunty at Little Bangkok. I can picture her eyes half-closed as she nods in satisfaction, savoring the creamy sauce. After she tastes my curry, she may even offer me a volunteer job at the emergency kitchen.

I let the stew come to a boil. Minutes later, I remove the cover and spoon up some sauce and a piece of the chicken. Like the chefs in cooking shows, I take a small bite. The chicken is just right—cooked but still tender. I sip a bit of the sauce and roll it around my tongue. It's rich and creamy, but bland. I stir in some salt and then add a few drops of lemon juice and fish sauce. I swish my mouth with cold water and take another sip of the curry. It bursts with flavor. I turn off the heat.

Knowing Aunty, she will inspect the whole apartment when she returns. I run around like a yo-yo, making my bed, organizing the books on my desk, folding the blanket on the sofa in front of the TV, and mopping the kitchen floor. When I glance at the clock, I notice that almost two hours have passed. I will have to warm up the curry when Aunty gets here.

"Food, food, Chinese food! Wok,
wok, iron wok. Stir, stir, stir-fry!"

"Hello, Aunty! Food is ready for you."

"Mei!" Aunty shouts through the phone. "I am outside the complex, but they won't let me in."

"Why? Who won't?" We don't have guards like at Ming's fancy apartment.

"I am sorry—it's a new order from the city!" a man says in the background. "You can't come in unless you live here."

"Mei, stay home. Don't go anywhere!" Aunty sounds frantic. "They set barricades outside your apartment complex. I will find a way to get to you."

THAI RED CHICKEN CURRY

Makes 4 servings

HERE'S WHAT YOU NEED:

2 tablespoons cooking oil

¼ cup minced red onion

4 cloves garlic, minced

2 tablespoons Thai red curry paste

1½ cups precut taro root or potato, cut into ½-inch cubes

1½ pounds boneless, skinless chicken breasts, cut into
   1-inch cubes

1 can (14 ounces) coconut cream

¼ cup water

1 red or green bell pepper, ribs and seeds discarded, cut into
   1-inch cubes

1 tablespoon lemon juice

1 teaspoon fish sauce (optional)

Salt and pepper to taste

¼ cup fresh cilantro leaves

HERE'S WHAT YOU DO:

Heat cooking oil in a large heavy saucepan over medium heat and swirl to coat. Sauté onion and garlic until fragrant, about 1 minute. Add curry paste, taro root, and chicken. Cook and stir for 1 minute.

Stir in coconut cream and water; bring to a boil. Lower to a simmer; cover and cook for 10 minutes.

Add bell pepper. Simmer for another 5 minutes. Season with lemon juice, fish sauce (if using), salt, and pepper. Garnish with cilantro leaves. Serve hot.

CHAPTER ELEVEN

天上九头鸟，地上湖北佬

In heaven there is the smart and resilient nine-headed mythical phoenix; and on earth, there are the people of Hubei

"Hello, Mrs. Fong! Did you get all the food we ordered?" A woman's high-pitched voice cuts through my window.

"I didn't get any meat, but I got your eggs." I recognize Mrs. Fong's husky voice.

With my eyes still shut, I try to go back to my dream. I was enjoying hot dry noodles, which were generously coated with black sesame sauce and flavored with pickled vegetables and chives, while Mother stood behind me, combing my hair.

"Thanks, Mrs. Fong. Here comes our basket," the same voice calls out.

"Okay. I will put the eggs on top of your vegetables," says Mrs. Fong.

I open my eyes, still feeling the warmth of Mother's hand on my head. Will Aunty find a way to get inside today? For the last four days, she has been bringing me food, but I want more than just talking to her through a fence.

"Slowly, slowly. Next time, attach the rope to both sides of your basket so it will be more stable," says Mrs. Fong.

"I don't have any more rope. Can you get me some?" asks the woman.

I look at the time on my phone—7:30 AM. I take a deep breath and kick off my cover, fighting the temptation to snuggle underneath the warm comforter again. Shivering, I quickly put on a sweater, slip on a pair of under-leggings and jeans, and run out to the balcony.

I cast my eyes downward at the makeshift gate set up at the right corner of the courtyard, between Buildings Two and Ten. Two tall, skinny men wearing blue masks and black uniforms guard the entrance. One has a blue cap on, while the other exposes his bald head. They stand side by side like a pair of chopsticks with one missing its top. How long are they going to lock us in?

Thunder rumbles in the distance. A line of black-headed seagulls drifts toward the Yangtze River, where rays of sunlight are visible. Is the one leading at the front the father bird? How lucky they are that their father doesn't have to go to work. Even though Father still calls and texts me every day, I haven't seen him for five days. When I ask when he will come home, he says he isn't sure but hopefully soon.

If it weren't for the virus, the courtyard would be filled with old people practicing Tai Chi, parents dragging their kids to school, and delivery people weaving through the crowd, carrying big bags of rice and packages. Now only two ladies are there, wrapped in disposable yellow raincoats, homemade plastic face shields, and surgical masks. I immediately recognize Mrs. Li's signature pink scarf and Mrs. Fong's one-of-a-kind embroidered dragon loafers, which I've only seen at the night market.

They are filling a bamboo basket with green onions, cabbage, and carrots from the boxes stacked around the rainbow bench right outside the playground. How did they get ahold of all this food when the stores are empty? The last time I looked at the neighborhood WeChat group, it was flooded with messages about ordering food, and I logged off right away.

A bamboo basket floats up past our balcony. I stick my head out and see that other neighbors are also watching the wobbling basket in the air.

"Be careful!" shouts Mrs. Fong.

"Where are my noodles and soy sauce?" a hoarse voice demands.

Without looking, I know it's Mr. Chen, who lives on the top third floor. Some neighbors call him Grumpy Chen behind his back. One time, I saw him confront Piano Girl's mother on the stairs.

"When your daughter plays piano, I can feel my bed shaking. What bad luck I have to live above you."

Piano Girl's mother acted as though she didn't hear him and kept walking. I bet that wasn't the first time he had complained to her. Now that I think about it, I haven't heard Piano Girl playing since the start of quarantine.

"Mr. Chen, I put your order in the basket. Let me know if you need anything else," Mrs. Fong says in her cheerful voice.

"Fine, but I want to pick up my own food. When can I shop for myself?"

"I don't know, but it's for everyone's safety that you stay at home," says Mrs. Fong. "Just let me know what you need."

Mr. Chen grumbles in response. I can't make out what he said, but I'm sure it was nothing pleasant.

Mrs. Fong now squints at a piece of paper and reads it aloud. "Mr. Wong, Building Five, Unit Three: one pound of daikon, two pounds of lotus roots, one dozen eggs, one package of noodles . . ."

"Yes, yes." The old couple who lives in the apartment next to us lowers a blue plastic basket from their balcony.

"I will lift it up and you can start pulling." Mrs. Fong puts a stuffed plastic bag in their basket and extends her hands above her head.

Slowly, the basket lifts from her hands, passes the garage

door, and swims in the air. Suddenly, it tilts. Daikon, lotus roots, and potatoes rain down. Mrs. Fong sidesteps to avoid the falling produce, but stumbles to the ground. Gasps and mutterings break out.

"Are you okay, Mrs. Fong?"

"Are you hurt, Mrs. Fong?"

"Did the rope slip?"

I run back inside, grab my N95 mask and coat, and hurry down the stairs. When I get to the courtyard, Mrs. Fong is leaning on a stack of boxes, massaging her back with both hands. Mrs. Li is dusting her off.

"Are you okay, Mrs. Fong?" I ask.

Mrs. Fong's eyes widen when she sees me. "Oye, Mei! What are you doing here? Do you need any food?" She grabs a bag of instant noodles from one of the boxes.

"No, I don't need any food. I came to help."

"It's dangerous outside. Go home!"

"Don't worry. I have a good mask on!"

I run around to collect the spilled vegetables from the ground. When I turn to put them into the basket, I almost bump into someone.

"Hello, Mei." It's Piano Girl, holding an armful of fallen vegetables.

"Hello—" My mind blanks. She has always been Piano Girl in my head.

"Juan, my name is Juan," she says behind her N95 mask, blinking her big, round eyes.

"Hi, Juan," I mumble, embarrassed I couldn't greet her by name.

"I thought you could use some help here." She bends down and picks a bruised potato off the ground. Her long blunt-cut hair swings behind her yellow knee-length puffer jacket.

Mrs. Fong brings over a few fresh daikon and lotus roots to replace the bruised ones in the old couple's basket.

"It's okay! It's okay! We don't mind," the old lady calls down.

"Don't worry, I will take the damaged ones home and cook them today," says Mrs. Fong.

I look at the lotus root in Mrs. Fong's arms. It has broken into three pieces and is coated with dust. Can she really eat that? Not wanting her to risk another injury, I grab the basket and try to lift it up. It's heavy.

"Mei, wait a minute!" says Juan.

I rest the basket on my hip and give her a surprised look. Juan knots the top of the plastic bag and then ties it onto the basket's handles.

"Even if the basket tilts again, the food won't spill out," she says, and her eyes crinkle into a smile. Was she always so smart? Why didn't I think of that?

Juan helps me lift the basket. We watch intently until the old couple pulls it over their balcony.

"Mei!" Mrs. Fong calls, still squinting at the list.

"Yes?" I walk over.

"I left in a hurry this morning and forgot my reading glasses!"

"I can read it for you."

"Thank you!" Mrs. Fong hands me the wrinkled handwritten list.

I read aloud while they divide the groceries into plastic bags.

"Building Six, Unit Two: one dozen eggs, two pounds of cabbage, one packet of instant noodles . . ."

After the mishap, the deliveries run smoothly. We are almost finished when a lady wrapped in a red raincoat runs toward us. Her mask, made from a big water bottle, bounces up and down despite her grasping it with both hands. I've seen this lady walk around with Mrs. Fong in the neighborhood before, carrying a little white dog in her arms. She must be another neighborhood committee member.

"I am sorry, Mrs. Fong." She sounds like a little kid who has done something wrong. "My husband said it's dangerous and didn't want me to come. We fought for hours. I finally got a chance to leave when he took a nap."

"Hello, Mrs. Wang," says Mrs. Fong. "Don't worry. My daughter says as long as we wear a mask and don't get too close to each other, we should be safe."

Mrs. Li chimes in, "We are almost done here today. Quarantine only started five days ago. People still have food at home, but we will get a lot of orders soon. We'll need your help."

"Can we count on you, Mrs. Wang?" asks Mrs. Fong.

"I came here to tell you that I want to help, but my husband won't allow it. I am so sorry . . ." Mrs. Wang strides away with her shoulders sunk.

I always thought the best part of being a grown-up is that you can do whatever you want. Why would Mrs. Wang let her husband tell her what to do?

"I can help!" I cut in.

"Me too. Mei and I can set up a WeChat shopping group," Juan offers. "It'll help manage the increased orders."

"Thank you, girls!" says Mrs. Fong. "We could really use the help, especially since we just lost a member."

Mrs. Li turns to Juan. "Have you heard from your father yet?"

Juan shakes her head. "Not yet."

For a brief second, I spot sadness in her eyes. I remember the sobbing and door slamming on the first day of lockdown.

"Is your mother still working at the mayor's office?" Mrs. Li asks.

"Yes, she is very busy."

Mrs. Fong turns toward us, holding two bags of food. "You girls take this."

Juan takes a step back. "No, thank you. I still have shrimp crackers at home."

Shrimp crackers? Is that what she likes to eat? Mother discouraged me from eating packaged foods since I was little. She said they were loaded with unhealthy fat and high in sodium.

I wave goodbye and say, "No thank you. My father brought me a lot of food."

The minute I get home, I search online for how to set up a shopping group on WeChat. Juan may be smart, but I can figure it out too. It surprises me how much discussion there is about getting food and setting up shopping groups. People have posted videos of empty stores all over the city. Where is the neighborhood committee getting groceries from? Is the city going to supply the food?

To my delight, it's easy to set up a WeChat shopping group. I even figure out how to set it up so members can send electronic payments directly to the neighborhood committee's account.

Afterward, I log in to *Chop Chop* and select single-player mode to advance my ranking. It took me months to earn five hundred rank points and become a one-star chef. I had to master the basic knife skills and learn how to properly wash and chop vegetables. When I let the boys use my hard-earned special cooking equipment, they bicker with me less.

To gain another star, I have to precisely julienne vegetables by cutting them into perfect matchstick size. To do so, my hands have to click the mouse, Control + C, and space bar at the same time. My fingers become so twisted, it feels like I'm playing a piano piece that I can't master.

I dream that one day I'll join the small group of five-star elite players. It might take me years, but I'll keep trying like Juan has done with piano.

> "Food, food, Chinese food! Wok,
> wok, iron wok. Stir, stir, stir-fry!"

I look at the screen on my phone. My heart skips a beat.

"Ming!" I shout into the phone. "Where have you been? How is Grandma?"

CHAPTER TWELVE

舍己为公

Sacrifice one's interests for the greater good

JANUARY 28, 2020, LATE MORNING

"Grandma's in the hospital," Ming says in a quiet voice.

"How is she?"

"Not good."

"I have some medicine for her! Can I bring it over?"

"There is no need; she can't eat or drink anymore."

Guilt washes over me. If only I had made it to his apartment before the ambulance.

"I am so sorry about Grandma, Ming. Are you okay?" I ask softly. "I was there and saw you get in the ambulance."

"Yes, they took us all to the hospital to get tested." Ming pauses, choking on his words. "We're fine, but m-my father wants us to leave with the American . . . evacuation plane, but my mother wants to stay to take care of Grandma, and I . . . want to stay with her."

"Do you want to meet . . . ?" I look out the window, calculating where I can slip past the fence.

"They closed up our neighborhood. No one can get out."

I try to think of something to say to lift his spirits.

Ping! A Discord notification.

TigerHong:
Wanna play Chop Chop?

That's it! Computer games always cheer me up.

"Ming, let's play *Chop Chop*. You'll feel better after killing some zombies."

"I don't know . . ."

"C'mon! It'll take your mind off things."

"Okay. You go ahead. I will join you in a bit."

"I can talk more if you want."

"No, it's fine. See you soon." Ming hangs up.

I send a message to Hong.

EmpressMei:
Yah, I'll be there.

TigerHong:

I'm playing with two guests. You can join anytime.

I turn on invisible spectator mode and join them, curious about how they're doing. The two guest players, Steamer and Meatball, are from Hong's school, a grade below us. They have been begging to join our team. The boys are making kung pao chicken. Hong, as head chef, is cutting chicken. Meatball, the sous chef, dumps way too much cornstarch into the marinade. Steamer, the kitchen helper, pours the chicken into the wok before the oil is hot.

As I predicted, the meat sticks to the bottom of the wok and they lose the game quickly. I look at the full chat box. They have been babbling away like old ladies.

Hong sent a photo of himself in a Hawaiian shirt, sitting on a ladder next to the big aquarium in his living room, smiling. A goldfish hangs from his fishing rod.

TigerHong:

I'm bored . . . I caught all the fish
in our aquarium, twice. 🎣

Meatball:

I beat my annoying brother at every
ring-toss game. Borrrrriiiing. 🥱

Steamer:

I've become a ping pong CHAMPION. 🏆

My dad is too scared to play with me now. 😵

I'm bored too. 😳

That's when an idea strikes me. Rather than be bored at home, why don't we band together to do something useful? I could form a volunteer group with them!

As always, the hard part will be convincing them to go along with my plan. My thoughts slowly come together. I will make a proposition they can't refuse. If they join my volunteer group and text me photos of them helping in their neighborhoods, I will grant them access to my special equipment and pick a winner to play head chef every day.

The moment I send out the message, I have second thoughts. What if they damage my hard-earned cooking equipment?

CHAPTER THIRTEEN

众人拾柴火焰高

When everybody adds wood, the flames rise high

JANUARY 31, 2020, EARLY MORNING

When I walk into the courtyard, Juan, Mrs. Li, and a tall, slender woman with a pink mask are unloading boxes with handwritten characters on the sides: vegetables, frozen meat, and soy sauce. The air smells fresh with morning dew. Occasionally, the sun peeks out from behind the clouds, as if playing hide-and-seek, casting golden streaks across the playground.

Mrs. Fong is standing underneath Mr. Chen's window, cradling a stuffed plastic bag with a cabbage peeking out. Mr. Chen sticks his head out of his window. His messy gray hair droops over his forehead, and the bottom half of his face is covered with a checkered cloth that looks like it came from an old shirt.

"Cancel my order. I can't cook now," he shouts.

"Would you like me to cook something for you at my apartment?" Mrs. Fong asks patiently, shifting the bag in her arms.

I stand near her, waiting to give her the printed shopping list. I detect a strong herbal scent of pain relief patches drifting from her. Does her back still hurt?

"No! Just refund me for the items. Besides, I've tried your cooking and it's not to my taste. But if you can get me takeout from Double Happy . . ." Mr. Chen lets out a chuckle and closes his window.

Mrs. Fong sighs and turns toward me. "Oh, hello, Mei!"

"Good morning, Mrs. Fong." I hand her the shopping list.

"Oh, good. Thanks, Mei! I've been struggling to read the orders on my phone."

I make a note to refund Mr. Chen. I don't want to give him another reason to be grumpy. To my relief, it's easy to add or cancel orders. The hard part is keeping track of all the questions and requests.

Can we order takeout? I'm too old to cook!

Masks? Can you get us some masks?

My baby ran out of diapers. Can you get us some?

My cat is starving! Can you buy some cat food for me?

When can I take Bagel, my dog, out for a walk?

Can you get us some goldfish? My son
fished out all the ones in our tank!

Do they think I'm the Buddhist statue in Baotong Temple
that has the power to grant all their wishes? Yesterday when Mrs.
Fong told me the city could provide our neighborhood only five
items for this week—rice, dry noodles, soy sauce, frozen meat,
and cabbage—I posted them immediately in the group. Soon
the orders and more questions poured in.

Is it true that the virus has
spread to other cities?
Is it true that kids don't get coronavirus?
Is it true the herbal medicine Lianhua
Qingwen Jiaonang can cure the virus?
How much longer do we have to be locked in?
When will stores open?

When I asked Mrs. Fong for answers, she said to tell everyone to ignore the rumors and only listen to the central government, which is saying that the virus is under control. She
didn't have an answer about herbal medicine. I wonder if Father
knows.

"Mrs. Fong, can we give Mr. Chen's order to Mrs. Song in Building Six?" Mrs. Li calls out.

"Sure."

I follow Mrs. Fong and join the group. She reads out the list while we divide the items.

"Half a pound of beef, two cabbages, one bottle of soy sauce, three packages of . . . uh . . . noodles, and another package of noodles."

The pink mask lady looks at the shopping list over Mrs. Fong's shoulder and exclaims, "Wow! All this is for Mrs. Song? Just days ago, she told me she had stocked enough food to last her family a month."

"People are panicking and hoarding food," says Mrs. Li. "Last week we had just ten orders, but this week we have twenty-five."

"I am getting concerned about people like Mr. Chen who can't cook for themselves," says Mrs. Fong.

Ding! Ding! Ding!

A series of WeChat messages come in. I check my phone.

Meatball sent a photo of himself standing in front of a delivery truck, holding a box of green beans.

Meatball:
@EmpressMei: You have to pick me as
the head chef for today! 😱 💪

Steamer sent a photo of himself holding four stuffed plastic bags.

Steamer:

@EmpressMei: I should be the winner! 🏅

I helped deliver 20 boxes of cabbage. 😄

Meatball:

I HATE cabbage. My mom makes us

eat it every day . . . 😭 😭 😭

I'm really glad they've accepted my plan and are working hard. But even though I know it's for a good cause, I am still dreading giving up my head chef position. I can't imagine what it'd be like working as a kitchen helper under Chef Meatball.

TigerHong:

We need cooked food. A little boy said his

grandpa is too sick to cook for him.

DragonMing:

Same here. Two neighbors said

they're too old to cook.

Steamer:

We got a shipment of frozen dumplings.
I could share some with you, but I can't
get out without a volunteer pass.

DragonMing:

I have one. Bc we had to deliver to some
families outside our neighborhood.

"Mei, Juan, can you take these orders to Building Two and Building Six?" Mrs. Fong points at two plastic bags on the ground.

"Sure." I reach for one of the bags, but Juan snatches it up. My arm freezes in the air. Puzzled, I look at her.

"Let me take this one. It's heavy!" she says.

Buildings Two and Six are located on opposite ends of the complex. As we approach the makeshift gate, I switch the bag to my other hand. The two guards are nowhere to be seen. Since the start of lockdown, when Aunty is too busy to bring me food, she has the delivery driver drop it off at the gate. Whenever the friendly capless guard sees me, he greets me warmly and brings me the food right away.

Juan calls out, "See you soon, Mei!"

I wave at her and watch her turn right and wobble toward Building Two. Her right shoulder is dragged down by the weight of the bag, making one of her legs look shorter than the other.

When I arrive at Building Six, people are already standing on their balconies, holding their empty baskets, bags, and buckets. Now the center of attention, I wish I could have carried a few more orders with me.

"Mrs. Wong Hua, I have your order," I call out.

"Here!" A tall girl in a bright red sweater answers from a balcony on the second floor. As she lowers a basket tied with a green plastic rope, her bushy bangs flop over her forehead. I take hold of the edge of the bamboo basket and put the order in. Like Juan, I tie the plastic bag to the handles of the basket.

"You can pull it up now," I call out. A woman with the same deep-sunk eyes as the girl appears next to her and wraps a red down jacket around her shoulders.

"Thanks, Mom!" The girl smiles at the woman.

A pang of jealousy and sadness stirs in my chest. Mother always worried that I was cold. Whenever she picked me up from night class, she brought a jacket for me.

The girl pulls up the basket. Her mother retrieves the bag of food and they both wave goodbye to me.

Pleased that my first delivery went smoothly, I rejoin the group.

As soon as Mrs. Fong sees me, she says, "Mei, delete Zhang Wei's and Tao Pang's orders from the shopping list. They just messaged me to say that they're too sick to cook." She sighs. "I wish our committee had the ability to prepare food for them."

An idea flashes through my mind. Why didn't I think of it before?

"Maybe the emergency kitchen can help," I blurt out.

"That's a great idea, Mei!" exclaims Mrs. Li.

"Isn't your aunt the director there?" asks Mrs. Fong.

"Yes! I'll ask her tonight!"

After dinner, instead of logging on to play *Chop Chop*, I rehearse what I will say when Aunty calls, which is usually around 8:00 PM after the kitchen sends out its last batch of meals.

"Food, food, Chinese food! Wok,
wok, iron wok. Stir, stir, stir-fry!"

"Mei, did you get the dinner?" Aunty sounds as if she's in a hurry.

"Yes. It was delicious. Thanks, Aunty!"

"Good. I am still at the kitchen and need to meet a supplier soon."

"Wait, Aunty! Some neighbors here can't cook for themselves. Can the emergency kitchen also provide meals for them?" I ask quickly.

She pauses, then says, "I'm not sure. The kitchen was set up to cook for frontline medical workers."

"But the people here need to eat too." I regret my tone instantly. Aunty hates being challenged. "Do you have any leftover food?" I ask in a small voice.

"Mei, that's not the issue." Aunty sounds agitated. "We have extra food from all the donations. It's that I only have so many hours in a day."

"Aunty, if you let me volunteer in the kitchen, I can take orders, help cook and pack meals. And my Phoenix Group can deliver them." I hope she can see that I have thought everything through.

"I don't think so. It's too dangerous for you to be out. What Phoenix Group?"

I tell her about the volunteer group I formed with my friends and how we've been helping deliver groceries in our neighborhoods.

The line falls silent. Desperate, I add, "Aunty, if I work in the kitchen, I can be with you every day. And you know I can cook." I hold my breath and wait.

Finally, Aunty says, "If I let you come, you have to follow *all* the safety procedures. I can't let too many people come to the kitchen. But I can have the driver drop off the meals for your group at the back gate of the Yangtze Hospital during his delivery run."

I've wanted this so much. I press the phone even tighter against my ear and say eagerly, "Yes, Aunty! I will do whatever you say."

"All right then. I will message you a volunteer pass and give you an orientation tomorrow. Be at the kitchen at noon. Wear your N95 mask and I'll have a face shield ready for you." Aunty hangs up.

I let out a happy squeal. At last, I can be helpful, spend time with Aunty, and cook with Chef Ma!

But suddenly, I realize I have a problem. Even though the hospital is within walking distance, the Phoenix Group can't get out of their neighborhoods. How will they pick up the meals from the back gate of the hospital?

CHAPTER FOURTEEN

灯不拨不亮，理不辩不明

An oil lamp becomes brighter after rubbing; an idea becomes clearer after conversing

JANUARY 31, 2020, EVENING

I log on to the Discord group right when the boys have finished a round of *Chop Chop*. I had picked Ming to play head chef earlier that day.

> **Steamer:**
> Where's Mei? We wouldn't have lost
> last round if she was here . . .

> **DragonMing:**
> She is probably busy volunteering. 🐝

TigerHong:

I gave my last bag of chips to the little boy with a sick grandpa. He was so hungry. ☹

Meatball:

I brought the old lady next door some of my mother's cooking. But I can't do it every day. We barely have enough. My younger brother is a nonstop eating MACHINE. 🍙 🍜 🌮

DragonMing:

Is there anything more we can do?

EmpressMei:

Yes, there is!

I quickly explain that I will volunteer at Aunty's emergency kitchen, which can also provide meals for neighbors in need.

Steamer:

You're gonna cook with a real chef?? 🙌 🔍
Can you get us in?
Your Aunty is a big shot there right?

EmpressMei:

No, sorry. But you can help deliver the meals. 📦
The driver can drop them off at the hospital's
back gate. We just need to figure out
how you guys can get the meals. 🤔

DragonMing:

I can pick up the meals and drop them off
to everyone. I have a volunteer pass and my
electric moped has a big luggage rack.

EmpressMei:

Oh, my gosh, I forgot you have a
pass. That's super! 😺 🙌

Meatball:

I'm in! 👍

TigerHong:

Me too! Can't wait to bring the meals to
the little boy and his grandpa. 😻 😄

EmpressMei:

Good. Just message me the number of
meals you need for your neighborhood,
and I will get them ready for the driver.

Later that night, I send Ming a private message.

EmpressMei:

Thanks for saving the day! How's Grandma?

DragonMing:

Glad I can help. She is still in the hospital,
but can eat and drink now. 😌

CHAPTER FIFTEEN

千里之行，始于足下

A journey of a thousand miles begins with a single step

FEBRUARY 2, 2020, EARLY MORNING

I woke up a few times last night, worried I would be late for my first day working at the emergency kitchen. Yesterday, I met Aunty there. She explained the safety procedures and introduced me to everyone. Chef Ma was very happy to see me.

At the gate, I show my volunteer pass to the guards, who are wrapped in heavy blue coats. While the taller one unlocks the gate, I check the time again—7:00 AM. I have plenty of time to make it to my 7:30 AM shift.

Treading the quiet and empty streets, I feel as if I'm walking in a deserted city from *Chop Chop*, where zombies will jump out from boarded-up store windows any moment. The ground is wet and sticky from last night's rain. I brace against the northern wind, feeling a hundred needles piercing through my jeans, poking my skin. I can't remember ever feeling this cold in Wuhan. Could it be because the street is usually crowded with people, cars, and bicycles? Or because I never get up so early?

For the fifth time, I tally the meals in my head: seventeen meals for the boys' neighborhoods and three for Mr. Chen, Zhang Wei, and Tao Pang.

My phone rings as I pass the Golden Seafood Market, now blocked off with iron fences.

"Food, food, Chinese food! Wok,
wok, iron wok. Stir, stir, stir-fry!"

"Hi, Dad!"

"Are you at the kitchen?" he asks. I hear beeping in the background.

"No, I'm on my way." I continue walking. "Is that a respiratory machine?"

"Yes. Are you wearing your mask?"

"Yes, Dad!"

"Make sure you disinfect everything when you get home!"

"Yes, Dad. Gotta go. Talk to you tonight."

When I first told Father I was going to volunteer at the kitchen, he was not happy and said it was too risky. I retorted by saying his job is more dangerous than cooking. Still, he insisted I stay home. Finally, I told him Aunty would be there to keep an eye on me.

He chuckled and said, "All right then. I'm sure she will."

Even though they don't get along, I could tell from his voice that he was relieved I would be with Aunty.

The wind lessens after I turn onto Victory Road. I can see the red flag above the school gate flapping in the breeze through the morning fog. It seems so long ago that students were swarming in front of the school, horsing around the vendors who were selling roasted peanuts, chestnuts, and rice-sesame candies. I wonder what my classmates are doing these days. Are they still studying hard for the Gaokao?

I spot Aunty outside the gate, talking to two men who are unloading a big bamboo basket from a truck. Boxes of supplies are piled around them.

"Don't put the frozen fish on top of the bitter melons." Aunty sounds frustrated. "You're crushing them. Wait, wait! Bring in the trays of tofu first."

Unlike Mother, Aunty gets frustrated easily, which sometimes makes me nervous around her. Knowing she will be furious if she sees me without my face shield, I snatch it from my backpack, put it on, and slide through the side door.

I set my backpack on the wooden shelf, spray my shoes with

alcohol, and wash my hands at the sanitization station next to the door. A hose snakes its way from the courtyard through the window and connects to a small plastic sink. A piece of paper with Aunty's handwriting is taped on the wall, above the bottles of soap on the windowsill.

> To keep yourself and everyone around
> you safe, please follow the rules below
> before entering the kitchen:
> • Put on your mask and face shield
> • Spray the bottom of your shoes with alcohol
> • Wash your hands for 20 seconds

As I scrub my hands, I sing the first part of "Morning Sun" in my head. Aunty told me she timed it to be exactly twenty seconds long.

> You are my little rice cake, like
> the morning sun in the sky.
> Your warm light shines on earth.
> You bring us hope and joy . . .

I dry my hands on a paper towel and skip into the kitchen. Steam penetrates the pores of my face. I breathe in the aroma of cooked noodles, which intertwines with savory chili, garlic, and sesame oil. I still can't believe I'm here.

"Good morning, Mei!" Chef Ma calls from the middle of the room. A white apron is tied around his narrow waist. He is folding and stretching, pulling and twisting, a fist-size clump of dough. A jade pixiu pendant dances around his neck. Like a musician playing the accordion, he moves his hands from side to side.

"Good Morning, Chef Ma! What would you like me to do today?"

I look in awe at the dough in his hands, now as thin as hair. He's making hand-pulled noodles. When I try to make them in *Chop Chop*, I never get past five pulls. The noodles break even though they are still as thick as chopsticks.

"Go help pack the règānmiàn."

"Sure!" I walk past a stocky young chef with the build of a football player. He is cutting a big pile of carrots on a makeshift workstation made of classroom desks.

I stop in the middle of the room near the stove—two burners connected to a gas tank. A wide-shouldered woman with short permed hair is arranging stacks of paper bowls on the auditorium stage behind her. The thick red curtains have been taken down and now lie in a pile behind bottles of cooking oil, sesame paste, oyster sauce, soy sauce, and vinegar.

"Good morning, Mrs. Liu."

She looks up, a thin sheen of sweat glistening on her forehead under her face shield.

"Morning, Mei!" Mrs. Liu greets me warmly. "Can you help add the toppings to the noodles? Of all the dishes we prepare for breakfast, hot dry noodles, règānmiàn, is the most popular.

I eagerly nod and take the bowls from her and set them on the workstation next to the stove. Waves of steam rise up from the big wok, curling like reed flowers in the wind. Mrs. Liu fills a small cone-shaped bamboo strainer with noodles and dips it into the boiling water. In less than a minute, she pulls up the strainer and swiftly dumps the thin yellow noodles into a bowl.

"Now, here is what you need to do." She takes a spoon and moves to the workstation, which is covered with bowls of chili sauce, black sesame paste, soy sauce, rice vinegar, minced garlic, ground Sichuan peppercorns, pickled green beans, and minced green onions.

She scoops the toppings onto the noodles as she calls out, "Two spoonfuls of soy sauce, half a spoonful of rice vinegar, a dash of . . ."

When it is my turn, I keep thinking about what the chefs on *Cooking Delicious* say — it takes only one extra spoonful of sauce to ruin a dish. I move as slowly as a turtle, desperately trying to recall the measurement of each ingredient. When I finally finish adding the toppings to the first bowl of noodles, snapping on the cover, and putting it into a to-go box, I let out a big breath.

"I'm sorry I'm so slow. I will get better." I quickly grab another bowl.

"Mei, don't stress yourself out. You will get faster with time," says Mrs. Liu.

Thankfully, the stocky chef comes over to help. After we pack up breakfast, it's time to prepare lunch. I find washing vegetables and packing meals are much easier tasks. For each to-go container, I just have to pack in two scoops of rice, one scoop of stir-fried vegetables, and one scoop of braised meat. I divide the meals for each of the Phoenix Group members into separate bags, then set them in one cardboard box. I put three more meals aside to take back with me.

At lunchtime, I finally get a little break. For safety, we have to eat alone in different classrooms and keep our masks and face shields on until the door is closed. I was a bit disappointed that I didn't get to cook with Chef Ma but I'm happy I helped feed people. After I wash and dry the pots and pans from lunch, my shift ends.

As I walk out of the kitchen, I WeChat Mr. Wei and Mrs. Pang to let them know I will put their meals in their mailboxes since nobody is allowed to go into other apartment buildings. For Mr. Chen, I will leave his meal outside his door and then send him a message to let him know.

Once I get home, I follow Aunty's instructions: spray my shoes and clothes with medical alcohol, hang my mask on the balcony to air out, and take a shower. I then collapse on the couch, but not for long. I take out my phone and search for how to make règānmiàn. I need to do better in the kitchen tomorrow.

I'm thrilled to find a video of Old Wong on JinQing Street. Whenever Mother and I visited the famous food street, we stopped by his stand first to eat a bowl of his noodles. We would always later regret getting too full, having no room to try other foods.

In the video, Old Wong uses different sizes of spoons for each of his sauces and garnishes, whereas I was using only one spoon in the kitchen. When the ingredients call for different amounts, I get confused and slow down.

I run to the kitchen, gather my measuring spoons, and put them in my backpack. Then I slouch back on the couch, close my eyes, and practice adding the toppings in my head.

Ding! Ding!

Hong sent a photo of a grinning boy holding a to-go box, standing behind a closed window. A few pieces of rice stick to his cheeks, and dark sauce is smeared on the side of his mouth.

TigerHong:
He said it's the best meal he has
had in a long time. 😬

Ming sent a photo of a man with gray hair showing an empty to-go box, smiling.

DragonMing:

He said it was his first warm meal in days.

RÈGANMIÀN—HOT DRY NOODLES

Makes 4 servings

HERE'S WHAT YOU NEED:

12 ounces rice noodles, fresh or dry

¾ cup Spicy Sesame Sauce, homemade (see page 124) or store-bought

¼ cup julienned cucumber (peeled, seeded, and cut into match-size sticks)

¼ cup bean sprouts (optional)

¼ cup chopped roasted peanuts or any other nuts you prefer

HERE'S WHAT YOU DO:

Cook noodles according to package directions. Drain and rinse with cold water to prevent sticking.

Place noodles in a large bowl. Pour the Spicy Sesame Sauce over the noodles. With chopsticks, toss noodles to evenly coat with sauce.

Garnish with cucumber, bean sprouts (if using), and roasted nuts. Divide into four small serving bowls and enjoy with chopsticks.

SPICY SESAME SAUCE

Makes ¾ cup

HERE'S WHAT YOU NEED:

¼ cup toasted sesame seeds or tahini paste

2 cloves garlic, chopped

1 green onion, green and white parts, chopped

3 tablespoons soy sauce

2 tablespoons rice vinegar

2 teaspoons sesame oil

¼ teaspoon fresh chili or dry red pepper flakes

HERE'S WHAT YOU DO:

Put all ingredients in a blender. Blend on high for about 30 seconds, or until smooth. Cover and let the flavors meld in the refrigerator for about 30 minutes or overnight before using.

CHAPTER SIXTEEN

一心不能二用

One can't ride two horses

FEBRUARY 10, 2020, MORNING

It has been over a week since I began working in the kitchen. I now feel like a little fish in a familiar pond. After watching Old Wong's video, I put various sizes of measuring spoons into the topping bowls. With the right size spoon for each ingredient, I no longer have to keep track of the measurements. I just need one scoop from each garnish.

I have become so fast that I can assemble a bowl of noodles in less than three minutes. When Chef Ma saw my progress, he nodded and said, "Organization always improves speed." Even though he didn't exactly praise me, a few days later, he asked me to assist him.

As it turns out, he is a patient and serious teacher. His voice is always soft and at ease, even when he has to go over the same skill dozens of times, like kneading dough into a smooth ball or dicing potatoes into even cubes.

Unlike chefs on cooking shows, he doesn't believe in recipes. When I asked him for an exact measurement of an ingredient, like oil or salt, he laughed and said, "A real chef doesn't do that. We cook by senses and feeling."

Today, we are making pan-fried dumplings. The last time we were making them, I was so eager that I snatched the dough with my wet hands. It stuck to them like soggy mittens. I spent hours picking off the white, scab-like residue.

When Chef Ma sets a big wooden bowl on the workstation, I grab a bag of flour from the stage and bring it to him.

While he is pouring the flour into the bowl he says, "When I first came to Wuhan, I had to tailor my cooking to fit Wuhanese taste: rice over noodles, moderate seasoning, less meat, and more seafood. But, in recent years, people here have developed a love for northern food, too."

Too nervous to respond, I hold my breath and slowly tip water from a porcelain jar into the middle of the flour mound. Chef Ma has said that this is the most important step. With a circular motion, he runs his bony hands just under the surface of the flour. The dough begins to clump, first in little florets, and then it adheres into one lump. When the dough forms into a smooth ball, I let out a deep breath and put down the water jar.

"Mei, don't forget to coat your hands with the flour."

"Yes, I won't." My face burns.

Chef Ma scrapes the dough out onto a wide wooden board sprinkled with flour. He cuts the ball in half. I dust my hands and take one of the pieces. Standing on the balls of my feet, I knead the dough with my palms, applying all my weight to it. I try to picture Chef Ma working on the dough as a little boy. Did he have to stand on a footstool?

I now have a sense of how he works. When we are at the crucial stages of cooking, he watches me like a hawk. Once we get to the easier parts, like kneading the dough, he becomes lighthearted and talkative, peppering in interesting stories from his past.

"You know, Mei, when I was your age, I also loved cooking. My family lived in a poor village in North China. My father was a village doctor and used herbs to treat his patients and cooked food to nourish them. I started helping him cook when I was eight years old. He used to say food is the best medicine."

When the dough becomes soft, I fold it over and keep kneading, using my arms, wrists, and fingers. It reminds me of making dough in *Chop Chop*. In the game, though, only my fingers get sore from pressing the keys. Here it's a full-body workout.

Chef Ma continues, "Neighbors invited my father to cook at their red-marriage and white-funeral banquets. At first, I went to help him because I knew I could get some good food to eat. Then I realized people were always happy around food, and I was happy when they enjoyed our cooking."

He now shapes his piece into a thick, long rope, pinches it into small, equal-size disks, and then flattens them with his palm. I follow suit. Next comes the challenging part: rolling out the wrappers.

In the past, when Mother and I made dumplings at home, we used the store-bought wrappers. I have been practicing making them in *Chop Chop*, but each time, the wrappers come out every shape but round.

The moment I grab the small rolling pin, the dough becomes the center of my attention. I make it a game in my head. If I can roll out every wrapper perfectly, Father will come home. And I will cook him the best dumplings ever.

Chef Ma keeps telling me that with practice I will get better. I'm determined to master the skill. I have been in a mad pursuit for days. I can't stop; I'm obsessed. Soon, I'm soaked in sweat. At last, a few of my ping-pong-size balls turn into an almost perfect round shape: thin around the edge and thicker in the middle, just a little bigger than my palm.

I miss half of what Chef Ma has been talking about and think the safest thing to do is ask him a question. "When did you come to Wuhan, Chef Ma?"

"Oh, I left the village after my father passed away. I wanted to build a better life for my family, so I opened a small noodle shop near the hospital. Once I had saved enough money, I moved my family out here." He keeps talking while rolling out perfect wrappers like a fine-tuned machine.

"People liked my restaurant because I followed my father's teaching that food is medicine. I alternated my menu according to the seasons: cooling food for the summer, warming food for the winter, rejuvenating food for the spring, and restoring food for the fall."

"What happened to your noodle shop?" I sprinkle more flour on the wrappers to prevent them from sticking together.

"I had to sell it to pay for my four-year-old daughter's hospital bill. That's why I went to work at Double Happy. But her respiratory infection got worse. Thankfully, I met your mother. She was such a nice person and a good doctor!"

I want to tell him she was a great mother, too, and how much I miss her, but I turn my head away so he won't see the tears in my eyes.

Chef Ma walks to the refrigerator and returns with a big basin. The meat filling inside gives off a delicious smell of chives, ginger, and sesame oil. We set about folding the dumplings. The first time I saw him making them, it felt like I was watching a video play at double speed.

Even though I'm not as fast as him, I can now fold them perfectly. I place the wrapper in my palm. With a wide bamboo spoon, I scoop a dollop of filling into the center, fold the skin in half, and then pinch the edges with my fingers. Like magic, when I open my hands, a half-moon-shaped dumpling emerges with the edge folded into a braid pattern.

A few days ago, when I made my first perfect one, I took a photo and sent it to the Phoenix Group.

Mei:
Look at this killer dumpling I just made. 🥟 😝

"Mei, don't ever let me see you texting while cooking again." Chef Ma's forehead furrowed, and his booming voice was loud enough for everyone to hear. "Put your phone away and go wash your hands."

Looking downward to hide my embarrassment, I stuffed my phone in my pocket.

Later that day, when I helped him dice daikon for the rib soup, he said, "Mei, remember, one can't ride two horses. Cooking is an art. You must put your whole heart into it."

Now he finishes coating a flat-bottom pan with oil. We set the dumplings in a circular pattern inside. It takes less than fifteen minutes to pan-fry a batch. When he opens the wooden lid, the delicious steam fans over my face. It makes my mouth water. The dumplings have turned plump and soft on top and golden-crispy on the bottom. When I pack them in to-go boxes, it takes all my willpower not to stuff one into my mouth.

"Mei! When did you get here?" Aunty's voice snaps me out of my thoughts.

"Oh, I have been here for a while." I look up and see two boys who appear old enough to be in high school standing behind her. The morning sun casts a golden ring around them, silhouetting their faces.

"Mei, meet the new volunteers, Jing and Yi. Take them to the cleaning station and show them how to do the prep work," Aunty says in her commanding voice, and then goes to talk to Chef Ma.

"Hello, I am Jing," the boy with a buzz cut greets me in a cheerful voice, shifting his gaze around the kitchen.

"Hi, I am Yi." The shorter boy with side-swept bangs waves his hand. A silver bracelet dangles under his baggy sweater.

"Hello," I smile nervously. "Follow me."

I show them around the kitchen and ask them to do a few simple tasks. They are much older. I assume they know more than me. But soon I realize they have no clue what to do in a kitchen. Every time I turn my back, they make another mistake.

Yi throws a knife into the bucket of soapy water, and Jing almost cuts himself when he reaches in to grab a brush. Jing drops a bundle of carrots still streaked with mud onto the clean vegetable pile. They keep apologizing as we rewash them all.

Just when I think I have run out of things to correct them on, Yi's baggy sleeve knocks over a bottle of soy sauce. When he wipes it off, a string of noodles catches on his bracelet.

But my irritation evaporates when they tell me they chose to volunteer after learning that some medical staff are surviving on instant noodles. I feel bad for them, not because they are clueless in the kitchen, but because of them being here. If not for COVID-19, this is probably the last place they'd choose to be.

PAN-FRIED
DUMPLINGS

Makes 30 dumplings

HERE'S WHAT YOU NEED:

FOR THE FILLING:

1 pound lean ground pork or beef

2 tablespoons soy sauce, plus more for serving

2 cups minced Napa cabbage leaves

2 green onions, minced

1 tablespoon peeled and minced fresh ginger

½ teaspoon salt

¼ teaspoon pepper

2 teaspoons sesame oil

30 round (gyoza) dumpling wrappers

¼ cup cold water for sealing the dumplings

3 tablespoons flour for dusting plate

2 tablespoons cooking oil, divided

½ cup water for cooking, divided

HERE'S WHAT YOU DO:

In a large bowl, mix meat and 2 tablespoons soy sauce.

Add cabbage, green onions, ginger, salt, pepper, and sesame oil with the meat mixture. Mix well.

Organize your work space with a small bowl of cold water, the stack of dumpling wrappers, and a floured plate to hold the dumplings. Cover the wrappers with a moist paper towel to prevent drying.

Dip one edge of a wrapper into the cold water. Spoon about 1 tablespoon of filling into the center of the wrapper.

Fold the wrapper over to form a half circle, matching the dry edge to the wet edge. Pinch the edges together to seal. Repeat with remaining wrappers and filling.

Mix 1 tablespoon cooking oil with ¼ cup water in a large nonstick skillet over medium-high heat. Arrange half the dumplings in a winding circle in the skillet; cover. Cook and simmer until the dumplings puff up and turn light brown on the bottom, 5 to 6 minutes. Repeat procedure with the remaining dumplings, 1 tablespoon cooking oil, and ¼ cup water. Serve with soy sauce.

CHAPTER SEVENTEEN

不怕慢，就怕停

Be not afraid of growing slowly, but of standing still

FEBRUARY 17, 2020, EARLY EVENING

With more people getting sick in Wuhan, now the Phoenix Group delivers double the number of meals. The kitchen is getting busier every day, but instead of cooking with Chef Ma, I still have to supervise Yi and Jing. I have been racking my brain for what more I can do to help them work better in the kitchen. Until, one day, in the middle of playing *Chop Chop*, a notification pops up:

Updated Tutorial Available!

That's it! I open a blank document on my computer. Like a running faucet, everything I have learned about cooking flows onto the screen.

KITCHEN MANUAL

HOW TO DRESS IN A KITCHEN

* Dress in well-fitting clothes. Loose sleeves can knock over bottles.
* Keep hair away from your face. No one wants to eat your hair.
* Keep jewelry at home. It can get tangled in food or pot handles.
* Wear comfortable, slip-resistant shoes.

WASH YOUR HANDS

* Before cooking
* After touching your face or hair
* After using bathroom
* After touching phone
* After touching uncooked meat or seafood
* After coughing, sneezing, or blowing your nose

A commotion comes from the courtyard. I ignore it.

DOS AND DON'TS IN THE KITCHEN

* Do separate raw food from cooked food to prevent cross-contamination.
* Do wash muddy vegetables before peeling.

* Do keep pot handles turned in so no one will bump and knock a pot over.
* Do keep the kitchen floor dry so no one will slip and fall.
* Don't put cooked food on an unwashed plate or cutting board that held raw food.
* Don't add water to a pan with hot oil. The oil will splatter.
* Don't use a knife until you learn how to safely handle it.
* Don't set a knife on hard surfaces. It will ruin the blade.
* Don't put knives in soapy water.

HOW TO WASH VEGETABLES AND FRUIT

* For firm-skinned fruits and vegetables, like potatoes, carrots, turnips, apples, and pears, clean with brush under running cool water before removing the outer layer.
* For leafy vegetables like cabbage, spinach, lettuce, bok choy, and leeks, submerge in cool water, swish, drain, and then rinse under running water.
* For delicate produce like mushrooms, bean sprouts, and berries, gently rinse them under a thin stream of running water.

I print out two copies and put them in my backpack. Outside, a woman begins crying. A heavy car door slams shut, accompanied by the sounds of windows screeching open and people chatting.

"Mother, Mother . . ." A heart-wrenching wail pierces the air.

I scurry to the balcony. What I see makes all my other thoughts evaporate. Red Sweater Girl is running after a white van with red block letters on the side—WUHAN NO. 4 FUNERAL PARLOR.

The van speeds out of the gate. The odor of gasoline hangs heavy in the air, overwhelming the smell of burning coal. How could this happen? I saw her mother just a few days ago. A chill slithers down my back.

"Mother, Mother . . ." The girl stumbles toward Building Six, wiping tears with the back of her hand. Like a ghost, she disappears into the dark entrance.

All is quiet. A bright moon illuminates the cloudy sky. A bird is perched on a bare branch. It looks at me and makes a mournful sound. When Father broke the news of Mother's death, we clenched each other for support. Where is her father? Is she alone? Should I go comfort her?

Suddenly, an ambulance races into the courtyard and stops in front of Building Six. Two men in white hazmat suits jump out of the van and unload an armful of wooden planks.

One man holds up a long board across the entrance of the building while the other nails the plank in place. My heart twitches with each thump of the hammer. What are they doing? Are they sealing everyone inside? My shirt dampens with sweat.

Soon the residents in Building Six realize what's happening. Some yell from their windows while others rush to their balconies and cry out.

"I haven't seen Mrs. Hao for days! I am not sick."

"Please, my father needs a COVID test kit and medicine!"

"We don't want to die here."

My sight blurs and my throat tightens. I stumble inside, feeling light-headed, as though the floor is swaying beneath my feet. With shaking hands, I call Aunty, but she doesn't answer.

Knock, knock, knock!

Someone is at the door.

CHAPTER EIGHTEEN

风雨同舟

In the same boat, sailing through a storm; working together to survive

FEBRUARY 17, 2020, EVENING

The knocking on the door continues. I freeze, trying to decide if I should answer.

A timid voice calls out, "Mei, are you there?"

I put on my mask and inch to the door. Leaving the safety chain on, I crack it open. It's Juan, wearing a gray sweater and an N95 mask. Wispy hair strands dangle over her red, puffy eyes.

"Hello?" I quickly wipe off my tear-soaked cheeks. Why is she here?

"Did you see what happened?" Juan wraps her arms around herself. "I am really scared."

"Come in."

I unlatch the safety chain and gesture her inside. It's comforting to have someone here. Juan slips off her flats and lines them up neatly next to a pile of shoes strewn on the floor.

"Did you see them sealing everyone in the building?" I ask as I lead her into the living room. "What's going to happen to that girl?"

"My mother said anyone who's had close contact with an infected person needs to be quarantined for fourteen days."

I think of Father. He is treating infected patients. Will he ever be able to come home?

"What will happen if those people get sick? They won't be able to get out." I gesture for Juan to sit down, but she remains standing. Her hands cradle her stomach.

"Are you okay?" I ask.

The fear in her eyes is replaced by a shrug of embarrassment.

"I ate my last bag of shrimp crackers. I—I'm hungry."

It takes me a moment to process what she's saying. She mentioned shrimp crackers a while ago. Is that all she has to eat?

"What about your parents?"

"They left the day of the lockdown." She blinks her teary eyes. "My mother hasn't come home from work. My father went to Zhengzhou to pick up my half brother, who has Asperger's and lives in an assisted living home."

"I didn't know you were home alone like me." Something stirs in my chest. At that moment, I realize—she's just as scared and lonely as I am. "Come, I will find you something to eat."

I lead her into the kitchen, searching for something more to say, but I'm at a loss for words. I envied the laughter that drifted down from her apartment. I pictured her cooking with her mother after I lost mine. I wanted her perfect life. I guess I was wrong.

We sit across from each other at the kitchen table while I try to figure out what I can serve her.

Juan looks at me intently and says, "I'm really worried about my father."

"Where is he now?" I ask.

"Trapped in a park. They won't let anyone from Wuhan enter the city." She scrolls on her phone for a few seconds, then shows me a photo.

A man with the same big, round eyes as Juan is wrapped in a multicolor blanket. Behind him, adults and children wrapped in sleeping bags, heavy coats, and bedsheets are spread across a lawn. Suitcases are split open, revealing the contents inside. In the distance, a woman is washing a blue shirt in a fountain.

How can they treat people from Wuhan as though they *all* carry the virus? Would these people have escaped the city if they knew they wouldn't be welcomed in other places?

"Can your mother help? She works in the mayor's office, right? Can she do something?"

Juan no longer tries to compose herself. Tears slide down her face. "My parents had a fight. My mother told my father not to go. They haven't spoken since then."

How I wish I had Mother's skill to comfort others or Aunty's ability to find solutions.

"I am so sorry. They can't just keep them at a park. I bet your father will reunite with your brother soon!"

Juan wipes her tears off with her sleeves. "Thank you. Can you keep a secret if I tell you something?" She places both elbows on the table and leans forward. Without waiting for my answer, she continues, "All the hospitals in Wuhan are full and they're running out of medical supplies and COVID-19 test kits."

I remember a video that recently went viral and ask, "Have you seen the video of the ICU nurse?"

"Yes. It was that video that encouraged me to volunteer in the neighborhood."

In the video, a young, round-faced nurse said that to preserve medical supplies, which are in dire shortage, she and her coworkers have to keep their hazmat suits on for the duration of their six-to-eight-hour shifts to prevent the suits from getting contaminated. She said that wearing an adult diaper is far worse than not being able to eat and drink. "My father has to wear a hazmat suit to treat patients. I am worried about him, too!"

Juan reaches over and pats my hand. "Don't worry! Help is on the way. My mother's office is in charge of building eighteen field hospitals. The first one, Huoshenshan, is already open."

My spirits lift slightly. With that many field hospitals opening, maybe they can stop the virus and Father can come home soon.

"Is it true kids don't get sick from this virus?" I stand up and make my way to the refrigerator.

"I'm not sure. My mother said it's more dangerous for old people, and so far only a few young people have been sick from it. But she still insists that I wear a mask when I go outside."

"I hope we don't get sick. What would happen if we did?" I open the refrigerator and then close it. I need something I can offer her right away.

"My mother said the new field hospitals are going to have the best equipment, and doctors are coming from all over the country to help. Plus, we can take care of each other," she says earnestly.

A warmth rises in me. I'm not sure how to respond. I always wondered what it would be like to have a close friend. With the boys in the Phoenix Group, we rarely have heart-to-hearts like this. I open the freezer and take out the curry I saved for Aunty.

"Do you like chicken curry?"

"Yes, I love curry."

I remove the plastic lid of the glass container, cover it with a paper towel to prevent spatter, and then heat it in the microwave. Soon the smell of musky curry and sweet coconut cream fills the kitchen.

Juan takes off her mask, inhales deeply, and says, "It smells so good! Mrs. Fong told me you're a great cook."

"It tastes even better when it's fresh." I transfer the curry into a bowl.

Juan looks longingly at the food while I place a porcelain spoon inside and hand it to her.

"It's sooo good!" she says in between bites.

My chest swells with pride.

I know that when people praise me, the polite thing to do is to say something modest, but I want to savor this moment. So many times when I heard her effortless piano playing, I felt talentless.

"I wish I knew how to cook, but my mother made me spend all my time practicing piano. I only know how to order takeout." She grins.

"Well, you're very good at piano."

Juan smiles proudly, swings a section of hair over her shoulder, and says, "I won third place in the last Yangtze River Piano Festival. But playing piano can't keep my tummy full." She scrapes the last bits of curry from the bowl.

I smile and hand her a paper napkin.

"Thank you! This is the best meal I've had in a long time." She looks at her phone. "Sorry, I have to go. My mother usually calls me at this time." She puts on her mask and stands up.

"Do you want more food?" I walk back to the refrigerator.

Juan looks at me shyly. I open the freezer and grab the last bag of dumplings.

"Here, you can have this."

Juan takes the dumplings but stares at me wide-eyed. It suddenly occurs to me that she may not know what to do with them.

"It's easy. Just drop them into boiling water. When it starts boiling again, add a bit of cold water. Repeat that process one more time . . ." Seeing her confused face, I say, "Don't worry. Call me if you have any questions."

After Juan leaves, I send her a text.

HOW TO BOIL FROZEN DUMPLINGS

1. In a small pot, bring 2 cups of water to a boil. Drop in the dumplings.
2. Once the water boils again, add ¼ cup cold water.
3. When the water boils again, turn down heat to low.
4. Let dumplings cook until they float on top. Serve hot.

CHAPTER NINETEEN

疾风知劲草

A storm tests the strength of a blade of grass

FEBRUARY 18, 2020, EARLY MORNING

I wake before dawn and wait impatiently for sunrise. It's a few hours until I can go to the kitchen to see Aunty. Still shaken from the incident last night, I think of Juan's visit and feel better. I must have dozed off, because when I open my eyes, streaks of sunlight pierce through my lacy white curtains.

> "Food, food, Chinese food! Wok,
> wok, iron wok. Stir, stir, stir-fry!"

"Aunty! I've been trying to reach you!" I shout into the phone. "Something happened . . ."

"I already know. Are you okay, Little Apple?" she asks.

"How do you know? I'm scared."

"The mayor had an emergency meeting last night with the community leaders. He briefed us about what happened in your neighborhood. Don't be scared. I'll be waiting for you in the kitchen."

"I'll be right there!" I jump out of bed, get myself ready, and rush out the door.

As I walk through the courtyard, I feel a strange sensation of being watched. I look around and see eyes peeking from behind window curtains.

"Hmph! Hmph!" A large man with protruding eyes loudly clears his throat at me from his second-floor window.

My scalp tingles. I speed up toward the gate. Do they think I will bring the virus back? Should I not be going out right now? If so, Aunty would have told me, wouldn't she? How did Red Sweater Girl's mother get infected?

The sky grows overcast. The last few leaves hang on trees that line the streets, refusing to separate from the branches like stubborn kids that won't let go of monkey bars. The chilly wind rubs my forehead and the air smells of smoke. On cold days like this, the well-off families warm their apartments with electric space heaters, while others burn coal.

The moment I step into the steamy kitchen, the rich aroma of ribs and seaweed soup puts my heart at ease. I look around but don't see Aunty. Jing and Yi are sitting on small, green plastic stools in front of a bamboo basket filled with muddy carrots.

"Morning, Mei!" Yi's face lights up when he sees me. Like Jing, he wears a blue tracksuit.

"Morning! I have something for you!" I hand Jing a copy of my kitchen manual.

Yi cranes his neck and reads it over Jing's shoulder, still holding a peeler and a muddy carrot.

"Oh, we should wash the carrots before we peel them? Aiyo! Why didn't we think of that?" Yi exclaims.

"This is great. Thank you, Mei!" Jing takes the carrot from Yi and puts it back into the basket.

"What's that?" Chef Ma calls out from the middle of the kitchen, setting a bowl of big yellow pears on the workstation next to the stove.

"Mei wrote a kitchen manual for us," says Jing.

I bring the other copy over to Chef Ma, who is now peeling a pear with a small knife. In a few seconds, the skin comes off in one long, curly ribbon in his hands. I hope one day I can master that skill.

Last week, Dangshan, a county of Anhui Province famous for its fruit, donated five boxes of pears. Chef Ma has been making nourishing pear soup, cooked with goji berries, lotus seeds, and rock sugar ever since. He says it moistens the lungs and eliminates phlegm.

He puts the pear into a big pot, rubs his hands on his apron, and takes the manual. I hold my breath and wait, wishing I spent time revising it.

Suddenly, Chef Ma bursts out laughing. "Nice job, Mei! I like this. Don't add water to a pan with hot oil."

"What's nice?" Aunty appears, holding her bag and phone.

"Mei wrote this kitchen manual." Chef Ma lifts up the paper to show Aunty. "This could be very useful for all the newcomers."

Aunty pats my shoulder and says, "Good job, Little Apple! I have to go to a meeting now. Let's talk when I get back."

Blushing, I nod and spot her chin-length hair hanging limp around her face. It looks as if she hasn't styled it for days.

As usual, it's a hectic day in the kitchen. I flutter from one task to another. After Yi and Jing wash and peel the carrots, Chef Ma asks me to show them how to cut them while he cooks the rice.

I first explain the safety procedures Chef Ma taught me, then I demonstrate how to dice a carrot: trim off the top, slice it lengthwise into planks, slice the planks into sticks, bundle the sticks, and cut them into a half-inch cubes. When I look up, the boys are exchanging confused glances. Chef Ma must see their expressions. He tells them to beat eggs and asks me to finish cutting the vegetables.

While Chef Ma heats oil in the giant wok, I pour in the beaten eggs. When the eggs puff up, Chef Ma pushes them to the side with his spatula. I quickly dump in the chopped carrots, green onion, and cooked rice. My hunger intensifies as the mouth-watering smell of rice, carrots, sesame oil, and eggs swirls in the air.

Yi and Jing hover around the wok, sniffing loudly through their masks.

"Can I have the leftovers? Just a spoonful?" Jing asks.

"You will have to fight me to get it," says Yi.

Chef Ma laughs. "After we pack the to-go meals, I can cook us more."

We first pack the food for the frontline medical workers and then for the Phoenix Group. Even with the additional orders from the neighbors, we still have enough left over for all of us.

At lunchtime, I keep thinking of the angry eyes in my neighbors' windows. I want to ask Aunty what will happen if I or someone else in my building gets sick. What will I do if they seal the gate of our complex? My thoughts jump to Red Sweater Girl. Does she have the virus? Can she cook? I decide to pack an extra meal for her. Aunty returns just as I'm ready to leave.

"Little Apple." She walks over to me and puts a handful of my favorite White Rabbit candies in my pocket. "These are for later."

"Thanks, Aunty." I notice I haven't smelled her peony mois-turizer for a while. Has she been too busy to put it on? I look up at her tired eyes and decide not to ask my questions now.

As if reading my mind, Aunty says, "Don't worry, Mei. If you follow the safety procedures, you should be okay. I will call to check on you tonight."

I hesitate, then ask the question that has been troubling me the most. "What's going to happen to the people locked inside the building?"

Aunty darts her eyes to the window and says, "The city will take care of them. After fourteen days, they can come out." She pauses, and then says, "It's best for everyone."

She helps me put on my backpack and walks me to the door. "Text me when you get home."

I nod and dash out of the kitchen. It's our neighborhood grocery delivery day. I am eager to get back to help Mrs. Fong and Juan. When I turn on my phone, WeChat messages from the Phoenix Group pour in.

Steamer:
Everyone loves the egg fried rice! 🍚 👏

Ming:
My grandma says it's the best egg fried rice she's ever had! 😄 It's the most she has eaten since coming home from the hospital.

I beam with pride and wonder if the rice will finally make Mr. Chen smile. Last night, when I left him steamed buns stuffed with pork and cabbage, he WeChatted me his usual dry thank-you and said he has hated cabbage since he was a little boy.

> "Food, food, Chinese food! Wok,
> wok, iron wok. Stir, stir, stir-fry!"

"Hi, Juan, I'm on my way home."

"Hurry! Something terrible is happening!"

"What?"

"It's Mrs. Fong."

CHAPTER TWENTY

三人成虎

When three people say there is a tiger, some will believe one is around

FEBRUARY 18, 2020, MIDAFTERNOON

Inside the courtyard, a group of twenty or so neighbors are gathered outside Building Four. Wearing a variety of homemade masks, face covers, and raincoats, they're craning their necks forward to look at something. Mr. Chen, leaning on his cane, stands near the front.

I run over to Juan, who stands on her tiptoes at the back of the crowd. "What's happening?" I whisper.

She grabs my arm and starts to speak, but a gruff voice interrupts her.

"We can't let her out. She will get us all sick," says an old man. A gray scarf is wrapped around his head and face, exposing only his eyes.

"Let's board up her apartment before the city comes to seal our complex. I heard her coughing!" cries a man with beady eyes standing in front of the building gate, waving his hands up and down. He reminds me of a panda with his greasy brown jacket wrapped tightly around his belly.

Last week, when I walked by Building Four, I heard him talking to Mrs. Fong loudly from his balcony, above hers. "You deserve a medal for doing so much for us! I don't know how we would get by without you."

A woman with wide-frame glasses and an N95 mask asks in a soft voice, "Can't we at least get her to the hospital?"

"Forget about hospitals! They're full for days!" a man yells from the crowd.

I look around and recognize many of the neighbors we have delivered food to. Why won't they stand up for Mrs. Fong?

"Hey, Dad, look what I found!" A chubby young man wearing a water jug over his head appears with a hammer and two boards tucked underneath his armpit.

My heart rate quickens. I take a deep breath and clench my fists.

"You can't do this!" I shout.

All eyes turn on me. Juan squeezes my arm.

"If we don't act now, we are all going to get infected! Let him through!" Old Panda calls out impatiently.

The crowd slowly parts, opening a narrow pathway to the

building. Face tingling and heart pounding, I try to collect my thoughts. Unlike the skinny young woman at the store, these men are big and strong. I'm no match for them. Suddenly, the image of the revolutionary hero Liu Hulan pops into my head. Wasn't she my age when she bravely stood against her enemies?

I bolt down the path. When I appear in front of Building Four, Old Panda's eyes widen in surprise. I block the gate with my body, stretching out my arms and grabbing the metal frame on both sides.

"What do you think you're doing, little beast?" Old Panda waves me away as if I'm an annoying fly.

"I won't let you seal Mrs. Fong's door! We need to get her help!"

"Help—what help?" Old Panda sounds even angrier.

The crowd falls silent. I can hear my heart hammering in my chest. But I stand firm on the ground and tighten my grip on the frame. In the distance, a dog's low-pitched barks intertwine with a baby screaming and a woman crying.

"Move, move! We got work to do!" Young Panda barks, making his way toward me.

Everyone stands still, watching. I feel as though I'm in a dream, an unknown world where I am no longer sure of the rules. But one thing I am certain of is that even with Juan's help, I can't stop them from plowing through the gate. And where is Juan? I look around and don't see her. Did she abandon me?

Young Panda is so close I can see thin scratch marks on his water bottle helmet.

"Stop, you dumb eggs. Nobody's sealing this door!" a hoarse voice thunders.

It's Mr. Chen. He jumps between me and the Pandas, resting his weight on his slightly bent front leg, while keeping his back leg straight. With both hands, he holds his cane diagonally across his body.

I immediately recognize the Shaolin stick-fighting stance from the *Kung Fu* computer game I used to play. Is he a martial arts master? Among all the neighbors, he is the last one I expected to stand up for Mrs. Fong.

"Are all your hearts being eaten by dogs? Why do you think Mrs. Fong got sick?" Mr. Chen points his cane to the crowd. "Raise your hand if Mrs. Fong has helped you."

The crowd mumbles and slowly all their arms rise. Old Panda rubs his hands together furiously like a kid trying to get dry mud off his palms.

"Well, what now? She's going to infect the rest of us!" a woman yells from the crowd.

"How do you know she has COVID? We need to get her a test kit to find out," says the woman with wide-frame glasses.

"Forget about it! The hospital has run out of test kits. My sister-in-law has been waiting for weeks," says Old Panda.

A siren slices through the air. Flocks of crows take off from the trees, flapping away in every direction. There is a commotion at the gate, and then it opens slowly. A white ambulance and a van pull into the courtyard. The siren abruptly shuts off. Like a pot of stew boiling over, panic breaks out in the crowd.

"They are coming to seal us in!"

"They are taking all of us away!"

"We are all going to die!"

"No, they are coming to take Mrs. Fong." Juan walks to the front of the crowd, phone in hand.

"Where are they taking her?" someone cries out.

"Huoshenshan, the field hospital that recently opened. It's well staffed and has plenty of medical supplies," Juan says in a confident voice.

"How do you know?" asks Old Panda.

"I talked to my mother. She knows because she is helping build the field hospitals."

The ambulance stops in the middle of the courtyard. Three people in hazmat suits jump out. One holds a handheld speaker and the other two carry a white stretcher.

A male voice blasts through the speaker, "Comrades, please stay calm. We are going to remove the patient and then disinfect the area. Go home and keep your windows closed."

The crowd breaks up and people rush to their buildings. I let go of the metal frame and move away from the gate. Young Panda drops his boards on the ground and scurries after his father. I pause outside Mrs. Fong's apartment and am relieved to see her slouching against the window. Her eyes dart around as if looking for danger.

"Mrs. Fong, don't worry!" I shout. "They are taking you to the hospital. You will be okay!"

Mrs. Fong slowly waves at me. Teary-eyed, her mouth spreads sideways into a smile. Mr. Chen and Juan come over and we wave goodbye to her.

I offer to help Mr. Chen walk back to our building. He rolls his eyes and says, "I am not that old yet."

Juan and I exchange amused glances. Once we are inside our building, I take out a to-go meal and say, "Mr. Chen, I brought you egg fried rice today."

"Good! I like fried rice!" he says in a cheerful voice I have never heard before.

COLORFUL EGG FRIED RICE

Makes 4 servings

HERE'S WHAT YOU NEED:

4 large eggs

1 tablespoon soy sauce

1 teaspoon sesame oil

3 tablespoons cooking oil

¼ pound ham, cut into ½-inch cubes

1 cup diced carrot, cut into ½-inch cubes

¼ cup fresh or frozen corn

2 cups cooked, cold rice*

Salt and white pepper to taste

2 green onions, minced

¼ cup toasted, crushed almonds

HERE'S WHAT YOU DO:

In a bowl, whisk eggs until fluffy. Stir in soy sauce and sesame oil. Set aside.

Heat cooking oil in a medium nonstick skillet over medium heat and swirl to coat. Pour in egg mixture. Cook, without stirring, until the eggs are softly set.

Break up the eggs with a spatula. Add ham, carrot, corn, and rice. Cook and stir until rice mixture is heated through. Season with salt and pepper. Garnish with green onions and almonds. Serve hot.

Note: Use cold rice for this fried rice dish so the rice will not stick together and get mushy.

CHAPTER TWENTY-ONE

祸不单行

Misfortune often comes in droves

FEBRUARY 18, 2020, MIDAFTERNOON

Standing in front of my window, I follow the movements of the three people in hazmat suits as they come out of Building Four. One person walks in the front and the other two follow, carrying Mrs. Fong on a stretcher. A white sheet is draped over her body, leaving her head uncovered. Her embroidered dragon loafers protrude from under the sheet. The chilly breeze sways a lock of her hair over the side of the stretcher like a strand of seaweed. The person in front opens the door to the ambulance and they carry her inside.

If Mrs. Fong was waving at us just a moment ago, why do they have to carry her? I hope Juan is right about the field hospitals and Mrs. Fong will get the best treatment there. The moment the ambulance drives out of the gate, four people in white marshmallow hazmat suits jump out of the van. Each carries a tank on their back and holds a cylinder sprayer across the front of their body. Like an orchestra conductor, the person in front moves his hands left and right, up and down, directing the others to different parts of the neighborhood. Soon, white mist swarms the complex. The sharp smell of disinfectant squeezes into the apartment, making my nose sting and eyes burn.

I run to the bathroom, wet a washcloth, and press it over my nose. Is this disinfectant poisonous? I want to deliver the remaining meals to neighbors, but I'm not sure if it's safe to go out yet.

A Discord message from Hong pops up.

TigerHong:

@EmpressMei: where are you?

We have been playing for ages!

Come play under head chef Hong? 😊

And good news! The little boy's grandfather

is better and can cook for them

now! You can take them off the list!

I only need 4 meals tomorrow.

Steamer:

@EmpressMei: I need 6. Two more

people in my neighborhood are sick.

Feeling cold, I wrap a blanket over my shoulders, put on my headset, and log in to *Chop Chop*. I need a distraction to calm myself.

> **EmpressMei:**
> Hey guys! 👋

> **TigerHong:**
> @EmpressMei: Finally. Where
> have you been hiding?

Should I tell them about Mrs. Fong? I decide to wait.

> **TigerHong:**
> @EmpressMei: can you show us again how to
> fold dumplings? It took us forever. 😖 🙁

> **EmpressMei:**
> Sure! Let me first tally the meals for tomorrow.

> "Food, food, Chinese food! Wok,
> wok, iron wok. Stir, stir, stir-fry!"

I look at the unknown number, hesitate for a moment, then answer.

"Hello?"

"Is this Mei Li?" an unfamiliar woman's voice asks.

"Yes. Who is this?"

"This is Nurse Yan. I work with your father. I have some news about—"

"What happened to him?" I interrupt, my heart tightening in my chest.

"He may not be able to talk to you for a while. He fainted . . ."

A chill rolls through me. Fainted?

"We are still investigating the cause . . ."

I gather my knees to my chest to stop my body from trembling. I can't register what she's saying. The busy tone tells me she hung up. I pull the blanket tighter around my shoulders and imagine Mother's warm arms around me.

I try to make sense of what I just heard. I don't know how long I sat there, until laughter echoes from the headset on the table. I look at the screen. The boys are rolling out dumpling wrappers. I type a message and log off.

EmpressMei:
Sorry, got to go. My father is sick . . .

I need to do something, anything. Should I go to the hospital? Would they let me in to see Father? Will he survive? Could I also be infected? I have been working with Mrs. Fong for weeks. Aunty, I need to speak to Aunty. She will know what to do. I call her, but it goes straight to her voicemail.

"Aunty, Father is sick! Can you please call me back?"

With shaking hands, I message Juan.

Mei:
My father is sick.

Juan:
I'm so sorry. Want me to come down?

Mei:
No. It's ok. Waiting for my aunty to call back.

Did Juan feel this scared when she didn't know what would happen to her father? Juan sends another text.

Juan:
Everything will be okay! Just like my father
eventually reunited with my brother,
I'm sure your father will be back.

Mei, you are the bravest person I know.

This is for you!

Piano chords echo above me, the final movement of *The Yellow River* concerto: "Defense of the Yellow River." Juan was rehearsing it for months and then stopped playing altogether after the quarantine began. Bouncing notes shift seamlessly to fast, powerful octaves. Gradually the vigorous music lifts my spirits.

When my piano teacher was preparing me to play *The Yellow River,* he spent half the class talking about the history of the piece and how Xian Xinghai, the famous composer, wrote it to represent the bravery and the fighting spirit of Chinese people.

Strength rises in me. I call Father and it goes right to his voicemail. I leave him a message to call me back as soon as he can.

"Food, food, Chinese food! Wok,
wok, iron wok. Stir, stir, stir-fry!"

"Aunty," I answer breathlessly.

"Mei, are you okay?"

"Aunty, Father is sick! I'm worried."

"I've heard. I'm making calls. I will keep you posted, okay?" She hangs up.

Right now, I wish Aunty would spend some time comforting

me like Mother used to do. Aunty, like the Yellow River, is temperamental and powerful, while Mother, like the Yangtze River, was compassionate and gentle.

Ding! Ding! Ding!

A series of WeChat messages pour in.

Ming:

How is your Father? Can we do
anything for you??? 😧

Meatball:

We can climb over your neighborhood
fence and come see you!

Steamer:

Meatball, stop with the stupid suggestions. 🗿👎
If we got caught, they would put
us all in a quarantine center.

Hong:

Mei, you can play head chef
tonight and forever 🙌

Ming:

Our team needs you!

Mei:

Thanks guys. I'll be back as soon as I can
and keep you posted about my father.

The piano continues. The fast and bright octaves increase in
strength and surge to the resounding final note.

CHAPTER TWENTY-TWO

水落石出

When water drains, the stone emerges

FEBRUARY 19, 2020, EARLY MORNING

After a sleepless night, I wake up in a cold sweat. In my dream, Father was playing erhu on a stage. Mother and I were sitting in the crowd. When I turned toward her, she was gone. The music stopped. I looked up and Father had also disappeared.

I can't go back to sleep, so I head to the emergency kitchen early, hoping Aunty will be there. When I step inside the kitchen, a whirlwind of white mist spirals from the stacked-up bamboo steamers, enveloping me like a warm blanket. Aunty runs over and wraps her arms around me. My body stiffens as dread overtakes me. The last time she hugged me was at Mother's funeral.

"How are you doing, Little Apple?" Aunty pulls back and looks deep into my eyes.

"I'm fine. Do you know how Father is doing?" I try hard not to break out crying.

"Don't worry, Little Apple." Aunty looks at her watch.

How can she tell me not to worry? Does she care about what happens to him?

Frustration bubbles inside me.

"Food, food, Chinese food! Wok,
wok, iron wok. Stir, stir, stir-fry!"

My body tenses up again. I didn't silence my phone. I look at Aunty. She gestures for me to answer.

"Mei?" Father's deep voice echoes through the speaker.

My heart skips a beat. "Father! Are you okay?"

"I am fine. I was just tired. I don't have coronavirus," he says calmly. "How are you?"

"I've been so worried about you." I fight back my tears.

"Mei," says Father, his voice heavy with emotion, "I am sorry I've been working so much and not taking good care of you. Your aunty told me you have become a great chef. I loved your dumplings. I'm proud you have grown into such a brave young lady."

I look at Aunty, who is smiling at me, fine lines deepening at the corners of her eyes. When did she bring Father the dumplings?

"Can you thank your aunty for getting me a COVID test kit? If it wasn't for her, I would've had to wait for days."

"She is right here." I thrust the phone into Aunty's hand.

Like a little kid holding a hot sweet potato, Aunty passes the phone from one hand to the other before bringing it to her ear. "Yeah . . . Sure . . . You're welcome."

With the tip of her boot, she draws a circle on the floor. I've never seen Aunty act like this. Is she nervous?

"Of course, we are family," she says, raising her eyebrows. Aunty hands the phone back to me.

Father's cheerful voice resumes. "Mei, I will be home in a few hours. I have to take care of something now. See you soon."

"I will cook something for you!"

I turn to Aunty and ask, "You brought dumplings to Father? I thought you didn't like him."

Aunty stops in her tracks. "Why do you say that?"

I bite my lip. After a moment of silence, I blurt out questions that have been plaguing my mind.

"You didn't talk to us for a long time after Mother's funeral. Is it because you don't like Father, and you're angry with me for not moving in with you?"

"O-oh, Mei," Aunty stutters, then takes a second to regain her composure. "I am so sorry. It had nothing to do with you. I was dealing with my own pain." Tears glaze over her eyes. "I couldn't face your mother's death for so long. And I was angry with your father for working so much and not taking care of you two. But now I understand. He and your mother took their doctors' oaths to heart."

She pauses, then pushes out her next sentence. "He did what your mother wanted him to do."

Like a bitter tea leaf dropped in warm water, any tension I had toward Aunty dissolves.

"Why didn't you tell me? Father and I were sad too." Tears blur my vision.

I imagined so many reasons why Aunty didn't talk to us. It never occurred to me she was hiding her pain. In my eyes, she was always strong and unbeatable.

Aunty takes hold of my hand and looks into my eyes. "You know, you remind me so much of your mother. When you didn't want to live with me, I felt I had lost both of you. I was selfish and wrong. Your father needs you too. Can you forgive me?"

I wipe away my tears with the back of my hand. "Of course, Aunty. We are family!"

"What are you going to cook for your father?" Aunty ushers me to the stove.

"Chef Ma says food is the best medicine. I am going to make kung pao beef with lots of ginger and garlic to restore his chi."

I heat oil in the wok and toss in a handful of chopped ginger, garlic, and onions. They make a happy sizzling sound. Soon, the tangy smell fills the air. I add a pack of thinly sliced beef and stir swiftly with a pair of long chopsticks. My breathing slows as the meat browns; I know that in a matter of seconds, the meat can change from tender to chewy. I quickly lower the heat, throw in a handful of julienned bell peppers, drizzle in soy-lemon sauce, and stir until the mixture is heated through.

After turning off the heat, I garnish the dish with nuts and green onions. I take a deep breath and feel my shirt sticking to my damp back.

Applause breaks out. Everyone is looking at me, and Chef Ma nods approvingly. I feel as if I have just earned the five-star chef ranking in *Chop Chop*.

KUNG PAO BEEF

Makes 4 servings

HERE'S WHAT YOU NEED:

1 pound flank steak or beef tenderloin, cut into 3-inch-long and
⅛-inch-thick strips

3 tablespoons soy sauce, divided

1 teaspoon lemon juice

2 teaspoons cornstarch

3 tablespoons cooking oil

3 cloves garlic, chopped

1-inch ginger root, peeled and chopped

5 dried red finger-length hot chilies (optional)

1 cup red or yellow bell pepper, julienned into 3-inch-long
and ⅛-inch-thick strips

1 tablespoon rice vinegar

1 teaspoon sesame oil

3 tablespoons chopped roasted peanuts

1 green onion, minced

Steamed rice or noodles, for serving

HERE'S WHAT YOU DO:

In a bowl, mix beef with 1 tablespoon soy sauce, lemon juice,
and cornstarch. Set aside.

Heat cooking oil in a nonstick sauté pan over medium-high heat and swirl to coat. Add garlic, ginger, and red chilies (if using). Cook and sauté until garlic browns.

Add the beef mixture to the pan. Cook and stir for 1 minute. Add bell pepper, remaining 2 tablespoons soy sauce, rice vinegar, and sesame oil. Cook and stir for about 2 minutes, until beef and bell pepper are cooked and nicely coated with sauce.

Sprinkle with roasted peanuts and garnish with green onion. Serve warm with steamed rice or noodles.

Note: To save time, use pre-cut, stir-fried beef and substitute bell pepper with other pre-cut vegetables to your liking.

EPILOGUE

苦尽甘来

Bitterness ends, sweetness begins

FEBRUARY 12, 2021, MORNING

The somber smell of winter has left Wuhan, and spring comes early. The trees have begun to sprout. It seems so long ago that Victory Road was as empty and eerie as a graveyard. Now the morning sun casts a golden hue on the New Year's parade. Dragon dancers lead the way. Acrobats jump and martial artists leap. Cymbals crash and firecrackers boom. The air smells of a mixture of sulfur from firecrackers, roasted chestnuts, and steamed rice cakes. Red lanterns swing above the bustling street.

People rush in and out of stores, which have red couplets pasted on their entryways. Arms loaded with gift bags, they greet each other with happy New Year wishes.

Juan and I hurry to Double Happy. A big sign is pasted on the door: SORRY, WE ARE CLOSED. HAPPY YEAR OF THE OX 2021!

I push the door open. Inside, all the tables are empty except the big, round one in the middle. A wide-screen TV on the wall is airing the New Year parade. Father, Aunty, Mrs. Fong, Mr. Chen, Mrs. Liu, Ming's grandma, and the boys of the Phoenix Group are talking and laughing.

Mrs. Fong sees us first and bursts out, "Mei, you look glamorous!"

Everyone turns to stare at us. I meet Ming's eyes and he quickly looks away.

"You look beautiful!" exclaims Mrs. Liu.

I nervously smooth down the sides of my red dress. "Thank you! Sorry we are late."

"Come here, Little Apple!" Aunty calls out, gesturing for us to sit in the empty seats next to her.

Chef Ma brings over a whole steamed fish that is covered with shredded yellow ginger, green scallions, and red chili peppers. The pungent sauce of garlic, chili, and sesame oil overpowers the other dishes on the table. Its smell reminds me of the sauce for the règānmiàn we made in the emergency kitchen. Even though it closed over ten months ago, the memory is still so vivid.

"Look! It's started!" Hong points at the TV. A lady dressed in a traditional Chinese qipao dress walks onto the big stage, where a red banner stretched across the top reads AWARD CEREMONY HONORING ROLE MODELS IN FIGHTING COVID-19.

The program was filmed last week to be broadcast along with

the New Year parade. In perfect Mandarin, the official dialect, the host announces:

> "Now, let's welcome the Phoenix Group and the
> young volunteers. These young heroes delivered
> food for neighbors in need and cooked for the
> frontline doctors."

She beckons us forward.

The camera shows a close-up of the Phoenix Group. Young children run up to the stage to present us with flower bouquets while reporters scramble to take our photos.

Aunty squeezes my hand, beaming with pride. If only Mother were here. She would be so proud of us.

The camera switches back to the announcer.

> "Dr. Li, the director of Yangtze Hospital's
> respiratory care department, will speak to us after
> the commercial. Stay tuned."

A close-up shot shows Father in his white doctor's uniform. Everyone cheers and claps around the table.

A detergent commercial comes on. Bubbles dance around a washing machine.

"Eat, eat, let's eat before the food gets cold!" urges Mrs. Fong.

Mr. Chen takes a sip of sour and spicy seafood soup and exclaims, "Mmm. It's just the right amount of sour!"

"Wow, the bitter melons are more bitter than the ones Mei and I cook at home." Father smiles and puts a piece on my plate.

"Thanks, Dad!" I grin at him. Father has become quite the sous chef.

"Everyone try the sweet eight-treasure rice pudding," urges Chef Ma. "Mei and I spent hours preparing it yesterday."

"Oh, good. Let's have something sweet," says Ming's grandma.

"Sweet, sour, bitter, and spicy—that's what makes a rich life," says Aunty.

I take a bite of the rice pudding and let the sweetness melt in my mouth.

EIGHT-TREASURE RICE PUDDING

Makes 4 servings

HERE'S WHAT YOU NEED:

½ cup chopped fresh mango

¼ cup green candied cherries, halved or quartered

¼ cup raisins

¼ cup dried tart cherries

¼ cup chopped candied pineapple

½ cup almond butter

1 cup cooked glutinous rice, also called sweet rice

¼ cup maple syrup, plus more for garnish

HERE'S WHAT YOU DO:

Line an eight-inch bowl with plastic wrap. Artistically arrange mango, candied cherries, raisins, dried cherries, and candied pineapple on the bottom of the bowl.

Pack half of the warm rice into the bowl in an even layer, following the curve of the bowl. Spread almond butter and ¼ cup syrup on the rice.

Pack the remaining rice over the almond butter–syrup layer. Flatten the top of the rice firmly.

Place a platter on top of the bowl. Holding them tightly together, flip them over. Lift the bowl off and remove the plastic wrap to reveal your fruit design. Spoon more syrup on top. Serve warm.

COOKING GLOSSARY

COOKING EQUIPMENT

Chef's knife: A multipurpose knife with a sharp, curved blade. It's used to cut meat, dice vegetables, slice herbs, and chop nuts.

Cleaver: A large knife that has a rectangular shape, used for splitting up large pieces of soft bones and cutting through thick pieces of meat. Chefs use its broad side to crush vegetables and spices, such as cucumbers, garlic, and ginger.

Heavy saucepan: A deep pot with a thick base and a lid, often used for sauces, stews, and soups.

Sauté pan: A medium-depth pan with a wide, flat bottom and tall, straight sides. It's used for multiple purposes, like searing meat, pan-frying eggs, and reducing sauces.

Skillet: A shallow pan with sloped sides and a long handle, used for pan-frying meats, dumplings, and eggs. It often comes with a lid.

Wok: A round-bottomed cooking pot with one or two handles, used in Asian cooking. Its round bottom heats up quickly and makes it easy for the chef to push food around when stir-frying.

BASIC CUTTING TECHNIQUES

When cutting ingredients, the goal is to create uniform, bite-size pieces so that all the ingredients will cook evenly and create an attractive presentation. If you are in a hurry, you can use precut fresh meat or vegetables. Below are four basic cutting techniques.

Dicing: Cut ingredients into ¾-inch planks. Cut each plank into ¾-inch sticks. Line the sticks up together and cut them into ¾-inch cubes. This cut is most often used for stews and salads.

Julienne cut: Also called the matchstick cut. First, cut ingredients into thin slices. Then stack a few slices at a time and cut them into the size of matchsticks, about 3 inches long and ⅛ inches thick. This cut is most often used for stir-fries or garnishes.

Mincing: First, julienne the ingredients. Then gather the sticks and cut them into ⅛-inch squares. This cut is most often used for sauces, pastes, and garnishing dishes.

Slicing: Hold the food firmly on the cutting board with one hand while holding the knife securely in your dominant hand. Cut straight down to produce even slices. This cut is most commonly used for grilling and stir-fries, as ingredients cut this way cook evenly and quickly.

AUTHOR'S NOTE

Since the publication of my first middle-grade novel, *Revolution Is Not a Dinner Party*, readers have been asking me to write more novels set in my hometown, Wuhan. For years, I was not able to find a story that spoke to my heart nor a character to whom I could relate.

In the beginning of 2020, I had my bags packed for a lecturing tour in Southeast Asia. My last stop would have been Wuhan, but I had to abruptly cancel my trip when coronavirus broke out and the city was put under quarantine.

My parents were both doctors, and I grew up in the hospital compound where they worked. When the situation worsened there, I couldn't help but wonder how my father, a dutiful doctor, would have responded, and how my younger self would have reacted.

I kept in close contact with family and friends and followed every development of the situation in my hometown. My heart ached every time I saw a photo or video of my beloved city in distress. Then I read about a young woman leading a volunteer group cooking for frontline medical workers. The bravery and selflessness of this group moved me deeply, and I decided I had to write this book to showcase the kindness of those who risked their lives to help others, and to show how friendship can give one courage in frightening times.

I began following a Chinese blog written by one of the young volunteers. I interviewed one of my friend's nieces, who volunteered to cook for medical staff. The image of Mei formed in my mind. Her voice emerged naturally, as I, too, know what it feels like having to act brave as a young girl, even when I was scared.

I learned cooking from my grandma when I was a child. Even years after I came to America in my early adulthood, I still dreamed of shopping in the morning markets with her. Cooking the dishes she taught me alleviated my homesickness for my beloved city, Wuhan.

The Chinese language is rich with proverbs—popular expressions that offer advice and wisdom, derived from literature, history, and philosophers. They are a staple of Chinese culture. Elders use them to guide their young ones, and young people pride themselves on how many they can memorize.

When I was young, I could recite hundreds of them. One of the games my older brother and I used to play at the dinner table was to start a conversation using only proverbs and see who could keep it up the longest. I always won.

Although the pandemic has touched everyone in the world, few know what life was like in the epicenter at the start. I hope this story will give readers a glimpse of how people came together in a time of uncertainty and panic.

My goal for this book is to show that a person's actions have the power to make a difference, that the darkest times can bring out the best in people, and most importantly, that young people can make an impact in the world.

Ying in her teens in Wuhan.

COVID-19

COVID-19 is a contagious respiratory disease that broke out in Wuhan, China in December 2019. At the time of this novel's publication, the origins of the virus are still debated, with some suggesting that the virus originated from the wild animals sold in Hunan Seafood Market. Initially, the Chinese government announced that it was not transmitted from human to human, but the virus spread rapidly.

When the hospitals in Wuhan overflowed with patients, ran out of equipment, and became short on staff, the government imposed a lockdown on January 23, 2020. Shops and restaurants were closed. Transportation was shut down to prevent people from leaving or entering the city. Masks were required in public, and people suspected of being infected were forcibly quarantined in their homes. The lockdown in Wuhan lasted until April 8, 2020. Two years after Wuhan's lockdown was lifted, new variants of COVID emerged. The Chinese government enforced a zero-COVID policy and placed many cities under lockdown, and Wuhan was under partial lockdown again.

COVID-19 spread internationally. On March 11, 2020, the World Health Organization declared the virus a pandemic. Countries around the world went into lockdown and mandated wearing masks in public. Vaccines became available in December 2020. At the time of this novel's publication, over 515 million people have been infected and over 6.2 million people worldwide have died from COVID-19.

ACKNOWLEDGMENTS

Thanks to all my family and friends in Wuhan for sharing your stories with me and giving me inspiration.

Thanks to my editors, Ann Rider and Amy Cloud. Thanks, Ann, for believing in me and taking on this book when it was still in its infancy. Your comments and suggestions are invaluable. Thanks, Amy, for your enthusiasm in seeing this project through and for your commitment to the book's success. Thanks to Anna Dobbin, Susan Bishanksy, and Erika West, the copyeditors, for your attention to detail and dedication to making each of my sentences perfect. Thanks to Samira Iravani, Kaitlin Yang, and Natalie Sousa, for your creative insight and stunning interior layout, and to Peish Zhang for your lovely interior art and Crystal Kung for your beautiful jacket. It has been a great pleasure working with everyone at Clarion Books.

Thanks to Stela Baltic and Hannah Shlesinger for your feedback, fact-checking, and proofreading. You make it possible for me to juggle many balls at once.

I've been lucky to have the support of the Trident Media

Agency. Thanks to Mark Gottlieb and Erica Silverman for your enthusiasm and dedication to the book's success.

Thanks to teachers, librarians, and booksellers who continue to share my books with young readers. It is your enthusiasm and support that encourages me to create the best books I can.

Last but not least, thanks to my husband, Greg, for your continued support and patience and for undertaking the drudgery of everyday tasks during the long days I worked on this book.